THE CHILDREN'S HEART SURGEON

BY
MEREDITH WEBBER

MILLS & BOON®

First published in Great Britain 2005
Large Print edition 2005
Harlequin Mills & Boon Limited,
Eton House, 18-24 Paradise Road,
Richmond, Surrey TW9 1SR

© Meredith Webber 2005

ISBN 0 263 18486 2

Set in Times Roman 16 on 17½ pt.
17-1105-55412

Printed and bound in Great Britain
by Antony Rowe Ltd, Chippenham, Wiltshire

CHAPTER ONE

THE music followed Alex from the ballroom to the bar—deserted now the dancing had started. The band was the best, seducing even the most staid of attendees at the congress onto the floor, and as his feet moved to the beat he felt vague regret that he hadn't brought along a partner.

He gave a huff of self-mocking laughter as he ordered a brandy.

What partner? He couldn't remember the last time he'd had a girlfriend for long enough for her to qualify for the word.

His own fault, as his last non-partner had pointed out, but she had been wrong about the cause. Wrong to blame his focus on his work.

What he couldn't handle in a relationship was emotional dependency. Put that way he sounded cold, which he knew he wasn't. But what woman would understand that he carried so many emotional burdens and expectations in his work that he was looking for escape from them in his private life?

Impossible, his sister had told him. In any good relationship there has to be an element of dependence…

He shook his head in denial of his thoughts and sipped his brandy, moving his head in the action just enough to realise he wasn't alone at the bar. Way down the other end of the horse-shoe, deep in shadow, he caught a glimpse of silvery hair, moving like a moonbeam on flowing water.

A woman swaying to the music, as alone as he was but feeling the lure of the beat in her body.

He hesitated a moment, aware that what he was about to do was totally out of character, then with great deliberation he put down his glass, stood up off the stool and moved towards her.

She was dressed all in black, which explained why he'd only seen her hair in the shadows, and still she swayed, unaware of his approach.

'The music's great. Would you like to dance?' He spoke quietly but knew he'd startled her, for she stopped abruptly and he could have sworn her pale skin turned even paler.

Behind him, he sensed the barman watching both of them—suspicious of him, protective of his female customer.

It was her turn to hesitate, but then she gave a smile so sad it hurt his heart.

'I'm not dressed for a ball, and I'm fresh out of fairy godmothers,' she said, holding out her arms to show him she was wearing black trousers and a high-necked black sweater.

'We can dance outside,' he said. 'On the terrace.'

Then he waited, willing her to say yes—willing her to dance with him because, for some unfathomable reason, it suddenly seemed important that she did.

He waited for ever, it seemed, until she gave a why-not, almost fatalistic kind of shrug and slipped off her stool.

He took her arm, tense as a steel rod, and led her out onto the terrace. Beyond it, manicured lawns led down to a large artificial lake, but the moonlight shining on the water was authentic, and the stars in the black night sky twinkled like fairy lights.

She was slim and lithe, and once she relaxed very light on her feet. In fact, she danced with a grace that made his dancing better—made him feel like someone from an old movie. Fred Astaire? Was that the dancing guy's name?

Her body fitted his so they moved as one, gliding across the terrace to the strains of the big band inside.

A moment out of time.

He was aware of that even as he held her in his arms, and an inner instinct told him to remember it, so he looked at her face, seeing a dusting of freckles across her pale skin and dark shadows beneath her eyes. He'd seen shadows like those under the eyes of his patients' parents. Shadows etched by emotional pain and physical exhaustion.

He held her closer, wanting to protect her, forgetting he needed to avoid emotional dependency.

Forgetting he didn't know her.

He was vaguely aware the real music had stopped, but he heard it playing in his head and danced on, knowing she, too, was hearing it— dancing to it. Then it started up again, a different tempo—slower, more seductive.

He felt her body stiffen beneath his hands, but he wasn't through dancing yet. Through holding her! Could he will her to open her eyes so he could see their colour? They'd looked dark in the shadows of the bar, but with her fair hair and pale skin, they could be light. Her lips were pinker than the skin around them, which wasn't saying much. No lipstick, but he could see their shape—their soft, ripe fullness.

Best he think about her eyes again, he told himself, but his feet had guided them to the darkest corner of the terrace and as the music slowed their feet stilled while their bodies kept swaying to the tune, as close as two people could be—two fully clothed people.

Seduced by music, and moonlight on water, and the feel of the woman in his arms, he bent his head and kissed her.

There was a long, indecisive moment as she again stiffened in his arms, then as suddenly relaxed against him. She didn't quite kiss him back, but didn't pull away or slap his face, indicating, he decided, by these two negatives that he could continue with this gentle, exploratory quest.

He could feel her heart beating against her ribs and sensed a tension in her, as if kissing a strange man was a very risky business even with two hundred congress delegates and their partners within screaming distance. And while he guessed she wasn't *not* enjoying it, she was also poised for flight.

Then suddenly she was with him, opening her lips to him, responding—whatever inhibitions had been holding her released.

Had they really kissed for an hour, or had they danced for longer than he'd thought they had? Afterwards he tried to work out the timing, but found he couldn't.

Unless they *had* kissed for an hour...

Could anyone kiss for an hour?

All he knew was that they'd kissed for a long time, demanding more and more of each other until it had seemed they'd known each other's blood.

Until he'd known they'd had to get off the terrace before they'd become a public spectacle!

'Can I walk you to your room?' he asked, voice husky with the passion kissing had aroused.

She leaned back in his arms, and looked up into his face. Dark eyes—brown or hazel, though he couldn't tell which in the shadows—scanned his face, while his own eyes were riveted on her bruised and swollen—well-kissed—lips.

'No,' she said, and pushed away from him, but as he released her he felt a shudder pass through her body, as if his suggestion had repelled her.

When she'd kissed him like she had?

Then she touched his hand and said gently, as if apologising for the shudder, 'My room's too far away.'

And with that she departed, not back into the bar where the dancers were now gathering for nightcaps, but down the steps towards the lawn, vanishing into the night's shadows.

He'd find her again, he vowed as disappointment doused the fire within his body.

The congress ran for three more days, and the hotel was closed to all but congress attendees and their partners.

Partners? He hadn't seen her at any congress sessions. She was with someone?

Married?

But unhappy—he'd felt her unhappiness from the moment they'd met.

He'd find her. Find out about her.

Kiss her?

That would be up to her!

CHAPTER TWO

'YOU know something, Henry,' Annie said, pouring milk over the cereal she'd piled in both their bowls, 'I hate the idea of starting this new job.'

Henry, far more interested in the preparation of his breakfast than in Annie's conversation, said nothing, prompting Annie to explain.

'I know I was excited about it back when it was first offered to me. Really excited. Well, all right, I was over the moon—but that was before I realised Dan Petersen was leaving. I thought Dan would be my boss.'

She lifted Henry's bowl and put it in front of him.

'Now I've got a new job *and* a new boss! And there's something dodgy about it, I know there is. I've been invited for little chats with just about every hospital executive, which, even when you consider it's a new unit, seems strange. And there've been looks between those pencil-pushers, and conversations that stop when I walk near them. Definitely dodgy.'

Henry gave a derisive huff, as if he didn't believe a word she was saying.

'Then there's the man himself—the new boss,' Annie continued, refusing to be put off by his lack of support. 'You know I don't listen to gossip—'

Henry's look of disbelief forced her to add, 'Well, I do listen, it's the lifeblood of the hospital, but I don't repeat it, except to you. And even if I didn't listen I couldn't have helped but hear the stories about him—they're legion. He may be a surgical genius but he's a tyrant both in Theatre and in the ward, and the words they use about him. ''Ruthless'' seems to come up most often. Now ruthless, as you and I both know, usually implies a person who'll do anything to get ahead, so why's a ruthless top US surgeon with an international reputation coming here, to Jimmie's, to work? Working here, even setting up a new unit, isn't going to put four stars on his CV—not even one star, to tell the truth—so why? That's what I want to know.'

Soft brown eyes looked into hers, but Henry offered no comment. Instead, he turned away, scoffed his breakfast then, realising she hadn't started hers, looked hopefully at her.

'You're not getting it,' she told him, 'so don't sit there drooling all over the floor. Go outside and chase a cat. Bark at something. Wake the neighbours.'

He gave her a look that acknowledged her contrary mood but made no move to offer comfort by bumping his big head against her legs. You've only yourself to blame, he was telling her. Or maybe she was telling herself, only it seemed more definitive coming from Henry.

'That dog doesn't understand a word you say.' Her father propelled his wheelchair into the kitchen. 'They go on tone of voice. Listen.'

In the sweetest, kindest voice a gruff and unemotional man could muster, he called Henry all the harshest names under the sun, berating him without mercy, while the dog fawned at his feet—bumping his head against her *father's* knees in utter adoration.

'We all know that trick, Dad,' Annie grumbled, picking up her handbag and looping the strap over her shoulder. 'I'll leave you two here, bound in mutual admiration, and go to work to earn some money to keep us all.'

Her father grinned at her, while his hand, twisted and gnarled by the rheumatoid arthritis which had also crippled his body, fondled Henry's head.

'Someone's got to do it,' he said, 'and Henry's got a full-time job taking care of me.'

Annie dropped a kiss on his head, patted the dog and left the pair of them in the sunny kitchen. Her going out to work to keep them all was an old joke between them, her father being well enough off to afford to pay for whatever care he might need and to keep her and Henry in relative comfort. But her father knew how much her work meant to her, so had encouraged her to continue her career.

'Or how much work used to mean to me,' she muttered to herself as she strode along the tree-lined street towards the hospital. 'Back when getting back to work was part of feeling normal, and having responsibilities in a job gave me a sense of being in control. Maybe it's the control thing that's making me edgy about the new position. Maybe I'm afraid this man will take that away from me. Maybe I'm not ready to lose control again…'

Two schoolboys steered a wide path around her, no doubt taking her for a nutter because she was talking to herself.

'A lot of people talk to themselves,' she said, turning to address the words to their departing backs.

The body she slammed into was solid enough to not only keep its balance but to stop her falling as well.

'Yes, but most of them look where they're going as they do it,' a male voice, enhanced by a rich British accent, said, and she looked up into the amused blue eyes of a handsome, well-built man, clad in an impeccable three-piece suit.

'Not necessarily,' she felt constrained to point out, backing hastily away from the suited chest. 'A lot of the ones around here keep their heads right down and mutter, mutter, mutter into their beards. If they have beards.'

She wasn't sure why she was arguing with a stranger over such a trivial matter.

Or talking to him at all!

She had to get to work. Start the new job. Meet the new boss.

'Being new around here, I wouldn't know,' he said, the blue eyes still smiling into hers in a disconcerting manner—a flirtatious manner.

'I've got to get to work,' she said, resorting to a mutter once again. Then she added 'Now!'

because her feet hadn't started moving in that direction.

'Me, too,' blue eyes said cheerfully. 'I'm heading for the hospital, and you seem to be going in that general direction. Shall we walk together?'

She could hardly say no. He'd come out of a house only four doors up from hers—a house that had been on the market for so long she'd stopped looking at the sign, so had missed the 'Sold' banner she now saw slapped across it. That made him a neighbour and to say no would be downright unneighbourly.

'I guess so.' Still muttering, though this time it was ungraciously. Now she had a new job, new boss and a new neighbour, and she hated change.

They were walking together now, and she knew it was time for introductions, but couldn't bring herself to take the initiative, feeling that if she didn't know his name, she needn't count him as a neighbour. She'd make idle conversation instead.

'You're going to the hospital? Visiting someone?'

It was early but the place allowed relatives in at just about any time.

'Going to work,' he said, surprising her, as she'd put him down as a lawyer.

'At the hospital?'

'I'm a doctor—a lot of us work at hospitals.'

She knew the eyes would be twinkling but refused to look as he turned sideways towards her and held out his hand.

'Phil Park. My father wanted to call me Albert or Centennial, but fortunately my mother's common sense prevailed.'

He dropped his hand when Annie failed to take it, and she could sense he was disappointed his little joke—which he'd probably told a million times—had fallen flat, but Annie was too busy absorbing his name to be smiling at weak jokes.

Phillip Park. His name was on the list of new staff—one of the doctors who had come along in the new boss's train. Paediatric surgery fellow? Anaesthetist? No, Annie was pretty sure the anaesthetist was a woman—Maggie Walsh.

Annie had personnel files of all the new appointees on her desk, but she'd purposely not read through them, deciding to meet the new staff without any preconceived ideas. Now she was sorry she hadn't checked. She'd known Alexander Attwood was American, but had assumed the other staff would be Australians from Melbourne, where Dr Attwood had been working for six months.

'And you are?' Phil was saying politely.

'Annie Talbot, former sister in charge of the neonatal special care unit at St James's Hospital and, from today, manager of the new paediatric surgical unit. Great way to start a working relationship—running headlong into you.'

Phil Park's hand clasped hers, warm fingers engulfing her palm, holding her hand just a fraction too long.

She withdrew hers carefully and moved a little further away from him, guessing he was a toucher, and not wanting to be the touchee.

'But that's great!' he said. 'We'll be working together, and neighbours as well for a while. At least I assume we'll be neighbours—or are you a health nut, and had covered several kilometres before you bumped into me?'

'No, we'll be neighbours,' Annie told him, though she didn't share his enthusiasm. Because, with the smiling eyes and hand held too long, she was sure he was flirting with her?

Or because the smiling eyes and hand held too long reminded her of Dennis?

'Manager of the new surgical unit, eh?' he asked, not in the least put out by her lack of enthusiasm. 'How do you feel about that—coming from hands-on nursing in the PICU? That is what your special care unit is, isn't it? A paediatric intensive care unit? And don't most unit managers come from a secretarial or management background rather than a nursing one?'

Annie breathed easier. He might rattle on but she'd followed his thoughts and talking work was much better than considering flirtatious new neighbours.

Or Dennis.

'I've mixed feelings about the shift from nursing,' she told him, 'but the new job's a challenge. The new unit is a challenge—I imagine that's why someone like your boss has come on board. Shifting to Jimmie's isn't like taking up a post at one of the renowned children's hospitals. We're just starting up. Neurologists and cardiologists—all the specialists, in fact—are still going to refer patients to the bigger hospitals.'

'Not for paediatric cardiac surgery—not with Alexander the Great on board,' he said.

'You call Dr Attwood Alexander the Great?' Annie was awed by such daring. Everything she'd heard or read about the man had instilled her with enormous respect for him.

Not to mention apprehension about the 'ruthless' part.

'Not to his face.' Phil retreated. 'But all of us—Maggie, Kurt, Rachel—use the title when we're talking about him. He's come here because of the opportunity to start a small specialised unit that he hopes will be used as a model for other small units. Other hospitals have paediatric surgical units, but they're not specialised to the extent we'd like to be. They do some congenital heart defects, which is our specialty, but they also do other congenital defects and things like brain tumours, gut obstructions, kidney and liver transplants—the lot.'

He glanced at her as if to see if she was listening, and as she was—and was fascinated as well—she encouraged him with a smile and a quiet, 'Go on.'

'Well, Alex hopes that if a small cardiac surgical unit can be made to work, physically, medically and financially, he'll have a model to set up similar units in city hospitals across the US. At the moment, over there, they have places like Boston Children's and Cleveland Clinic, maybe ten large hospitals with elite paediatric surgery units, but that means seriously ill babies, often newborn, with complex heart problems requiring surgery, have to travel huge distances for treatment, which not only puts extra stress on them but also disrupts family life and support systems.'

Annie took it all in—even felt a skip of excitement for the vision in her own heart—but at the same time his words puzzled her.

'Does anyone else know of this plan of Dr Attwood's? Is the hospital CEO on side? Does the board know? The government? After all, most of our funds come from them.'

She glanced towards Phil and for the first time saw his smile replaced by a frown. She hurried to dispel it.

'I'm only asking because, as unit manager, I hadn't heard any of this,' she explained. 'I thought we were going to be just another paediatric surgical unit like the ones you've mentioned.'

Her voice trailed away as she wondered if she'd missed something in the job description and in the interviews that had followed her application. Although that might explain the 'little talks' and her feeling that something 'dodgy' was going on!

'A number of people know,' Phil said, then he must have realised he'd spoken abruptly, for he found his smile again and favoured her with a particularly warm and teasing version of it. 'Though I've just committed the cardinal sin in Alex's book and blabbed about it to a virtual stranger before he's held his briefing.'

A pause, then he grasped her arm and added, 'You won't give me away, will you? You'll look suitably surprised and then delighted when he tells everyone at the staff meeting?'

They were walking through the hospital gates and up the paved path towards the main staff entrance as Phil made this plea. Annie studied him for a moment, wondering why an attractive, self-assured man should be worrying over such a minor indiscretion as telling a colleague something she'd hear very shortly anyway.

The word 'ruthless' echoed in her head. Was the gossip even half-right? Was the new boss tyrannical enough to cause his colleague such alarm?

She patted Phil's hand, still resting on her arm, to reassure him and led the way through the doors, nodding at other staff arriving early for their shift.

'Trust you to find a beautiful woman before you've even entered the hospital,' a deep voice said, and Annie turned to see another immaculate three-piece suit standing just inside the entrance. Inside it was a tall, rangy man, with a craggy face and the coolest, clearest grey eyes she'd ever seen.

Her heart stopped beating, stuttered back to life, then raced out of control. It couldn't be...

Yet she knew it was.

Had known it was from the moment she'd heard his voice...

'Do I know you?' He reached out a hand towards her as he asked the question, and Annie stepped back.

He sounded perplexed and when she glanced at him again she saw the untidy brows drawn together in a frown as if perplexed wasn't an emotion he enjoyed.

'No!' she said, far too loudly in the small space, then wondered if something less definite—a vague *I don't think so*—might have been more believable.

'This is Annie Talbot,' Phil said to the suit. 'She's our neighbour *and* our new unit manager. She bumped into me—literally—outside our gate. Your gate. Annie, this is Alex Attwood.'

This cannot be happening. That was Annie's first thought.

But it is, was her second.

The third suggested it wouldn't matter. *Might* not matter. Especially if she stuck to her denial. She'd just go through to her office, sit down and think things through.

After which she could find out about jobs in Botswana or Tibet or somewhere.

Except she didn't have a passport—not a real one…

'Dr Attwood,' she said coolly, gaining some control over her panic and finally responding to Philip's introduction. 'Welcome to St James's. Phil, I'll see you later.'

She strode away.

Alex watched her long slim legs eating up the yards down the corridor, saw her head move as she acknowledged colleagues and her hand lift to give a slight wave to others.

It was her. He would swear it was. The hair was different—but women were always changing their hair. He knew it was her from the way she moved. He'd watched her stride away from him once before.

And from her voice—low register, somewhat husky…

But he would also swear there'd been no Annie Talbot on the list he'd kept for the last five years. The most likely name, he'd eventually decided, after three days of detective work and straight-out gossip at the congress, had been Rowena Drake, wife of an Australian cardiologist called Dennis Drake. The fact that she was married should have stopped him thinking about her right then and there but, like the prince with the glass slipper, he'd wanted to know for certain who his mystery woman was.

Since coming to Australia six months ago, Alex had tried to find Dennis Drake, but though records of his training existed it appeared he was no longer practicing in Australia. Probably still working in the US, where he'd been five years ago, Alex had decided, and he'd put the matter to rest once again.

Now here she was!

Alex shook his head. He didn't know that. And she'd said they hadn't met. The odds of Annie Talbot being Rowena Drake—being his mystery woman—were a million to one, probably even higher than that, given the population of the country and the percentage of women in the figure.

Yet he'd felt that connection, and he would swear she'd felt it, too.

'Are you listening to me?'

Phil's question made Alex realise how deeply he'd lost himself in his memories of the past.

'Not really,' he told Phil, certain all he'd been delivering had been gossip about their colleague. Although learning more about her might help him…

'I was saying Maggie phoned just after you left the house. She wanted to know when you hoped to start operating. A colleague has asked her to stand in with him in a liver transplant later tomorrow, but she doesn't want to say yes until she's spoken to you.'

'We won't be starting tomorrow,' Alex replied, feeling better now he could focus back on work. 'I kept the week clear for checking equipment, staff training, talking to local cardiologists, reviewing files of possible patients and generally settling in. I'll be seeing Maggie at the meeting, we can talk about it then.'

He'd be seeing Annie Talbot at the meeting, too. Seeing a lot of her, in fact. But if it *was* her, and she'd lied about meeting him before, what kind of base was that for a working relationship?

'Who are you waiting for?' Phil had broken the silence again.

'Waiting for?'

'We're standing here in the staff entranceway, which, in case you haven't noticed, is becoming increasingly congested. You were standing here when I arrived. I assumed you were waiting for someone.'

'Oh! No! Well, I might have been waiting for you. Actually, I came in, then wondered about exits and entrances—not knowing the hospital—and went back outside to look around. I'd just come back in and was looking at the fire evacuation plan on the wall when you walked in.'

'You were checking out the fire exit plan?'

Phil's disbelief was evident and Alex wasn't surprised but, having seen the plan on the wall, it had seemed like a good excuse. He could hardly admit he'd seen Phil come through the gates with the woman, and something about her—the way she'd moved—the way her hair had swung to her shoulders, though it was dark, not fair as moonlight—had caused a hitch in his breathing and held him rooted to the spot.

'Let's go,' he said, refusing to be drawn any further into a totally pointless conversation. 'There's a small lecture room included in the space the hospital has allotted us. It's not ideal for staff meetings as I'd rather we were all on one level, but with space at a premium in all hospitals we were lucky to get it. Nine o'clock, we're on show. That's if your pretty woman has organised things for us.'

'She *is* pretty, isn't she? And she struck me as an efficient type—power suit and all. Though she told me she was head of the PICU before she took this job. Did you know that? Do you know of many hands-on nurses who've gone into admin positions?'

Alex felt his forehead tightening and realised he was frowning, though he tried hard to control this facial expression, knowing it made him look especially grim and therefore intimidating to the families of his patients.

'No, I didn't know, but I don't think it matters as long as she's efficient at her job. I did ask to be involved in choosing the manager—after all, she'll be acting as my personal assistant as well—but I was told in no uncertain terms they already had someone for the job.'

'You didn't do too badly, getting to bring your own fellow, anaesthetist, perfusionist and head theatre nurse.'

'It was a condition of my employment,' Alex said briefly, his mind, now they'd reached the fourth floor where the unit would be situated, on what lay ahead. He may have brought key figures with him, people who'd worked with him during his time in Melbourne, but for the unit to succeed it had to be a team effort. An image of Annie Talbot flashed through his mind. She would be both the hands-on team leader and his liaison with the powers that be within the hospital. The second element was as important as the first—in fact, it could be the key to success.

So he had to get over his reaction to her. Even if she *was* the woman on the terrace, she didn't want to remember it. Didn't want him to remember it.

Well, he'd tried darned hard not to, yet for five years his subconscious had measured all women against her.

Against a ghost.

A wraith.

A woman he didn't know!

Annie slumped down at her desk and buried her face in her hands. This couldn't be happening.

It was!

OK, so did it matter?

She took a deep breath and thought about that one.

In some ways yes, because it had physically hurt her to deny they'd met before, when it had been that night—that small experience of dancing with that man and kissing him—which had freed her from her living hell.

Kissing Alex Attwood, although she'd had no idea at the time who he was, had shattered the chain that had bound her to Dennis. Kissing Alex Attwood had made her turn away from the hotel room where her husband had slept, knocked out by a drug he'd been given for seafood poisoning, and keep walking until she'd reached the nearest town, where she'd gone into the police station and asked the sleepy man on duty if she could phone Australia.

Heavens! She should be down on her knees kissing Alex's feet, not denying she'd ever met him, but the denial had been instinctive, and now, she knew, on so many levels, it had been the right thing to do.

And, given that cardiologists and cardiac surgeons, even in a place the size of the US, moved in the same small world, it was also the only safe thing to do.

Having sorted that out, she raised her head and looked at the clock. Five minutes to the staff meeting and she hadn't checked the room. Hadn't done anything but panic since she'd seen him.

Again she felt the jolt of recognition that had shaken her body when she'd looked at the man. Could one body know another so instinctively?

After so short a time?

After one dance?

One kiss?

She shook her head. *Forget it. Get moving. You're here to work, and you're Annie Talbot, not Rowena Drake.*

Dragging air into her lungs, willing the deep breaths to calm her nerves, she entered the small lecture room, crossing to the table on the raised dais, checking there was a jug of water and sufficient glasses for those who would be sitting there—her new acquaintance, Phil; the big boss and the rest of his retinue; Col Bennett, hospital CEO; and herself. Col would introduce the newcomers, then hand over to her to introduce the staff members who would be fixtures in the unit—the unit secretary, two paediatric special care sisters, two sisters from the paediatric surgical ward and two theatre sisters. Other staff would be rostered through the unit once operations were under way.

She was using efficiency to block off any other thoughts. If Phil was right about Alex's plans for the unit, she'd need to focus completely on what lay ahead workwise.

'All ready?'

She recognised the voice and turned to see Alex Attwood, frowning grimly, apparently at her. Then, as if he'd suddenly become aware of his fierce expression, he adjusted his features into a smile. The expression shifted the planes of his craggy face so he looked not exactly handsome but very close to it.

Though it wasn't just the look, but a kind of power she felt emanating from him as he came towards her, that made her realise he was an attractive man. Not conventionally good-looking as Phil was, but attractive nonetheless.

Not that she'd considered attractiveness five years ago when he'd asked her to dance. She'd been too caught up in the music and in an illicit feeling of freedom to take much notice of him as anything more than a dance partner.

Until he'd kissed her...

And by then he'd been too close for her to really see much of him.

'I think so,' she said, wishing she could press her hands to her overheated cheeks but knowing that would just draw attention to them.

He was looking at the table on the dais, as if checking off who would sit where. Maybe he hadn't noticed her scarlet cheeks.

'I'm sorry we didn't get a chance to get together before today,' he said. 'I'd intended getting over on Friday, but a friend asked me to assist at the Children's Hospital—an emergency admission. Three-month-old brought in from the country with an undiagnosed PDA.'

Mentally, Annie translated the initials into patent ductus arteriosis. The foetal duct between the pulmonary artery and the aorta hadn't closed, so oxygen-rich blood was still flowing from the aorta back into the pulmonary artery and the lungs. It occurred more often in premmie babies and usually closed spontaneously, but if it didn't, it could lead to a number of problems for the infant or growing child.

It was a relatively common operation now, with good success rates. The best ever achieved in Australia had been during the time Alex Attwood had been in Melbourne.

'The baby OK?' she asked, and saw her new boss smile again—though this time with a warmth that had been absent when he'd used a smile to reassure her earlier.

'Doing great,' he said, still smiling. 'Just great.'

Annie heard genuine satisfaction in his voice and some of her apprehension faded. She had enormous respect for doctors who cared deeply about their patients. So with respect, and with admiration for his ability as a surgeon, she could shut that tiny moment in time when their paths had crossed back where it belonged, in a far corner of her memory, and get on with the job she'd been appointed to do. She was so pleased with this discovery she forgot her promise to Phil.

'Phil was saying you're hoping to make this unit a specialised paediatric cardiac surgery unit—a model for small units that could work in other hospitals across the world. Does everyone know this? I mean, the hospital CEO, the board. I'm only asking because no one mentioned it to me...'

Too late, the echo of the words she'd used to Phil reminded her she wasn't supposed to know, and the return of the frown to Alex's face suggested he was less than pleased with both her and his offsider.

'Quite a number of people know.'

The voice she remembered, even with the memory tucked away, hardened.

'And a high percentage of them are influential in both medical and government circles, but—what are you? Thirty-one? Thirty-two?—you must know how political medicine is. Hospitals have to fight each other for the best funding deals, fight for corporate sponsorship. If news of this unit had leaked out, there'd have been a furore about funds being diverted from other places. We needed it to be a *fait accompli* before making any announcement.'

He strode across the dais then propped his elbows on the lectern and turned to look back at her, as if prepared to lecture his audience of one.

'You'll hear all of this very shortly—and after that the word will spread and the fun and fighting will begin. But believe me, Annie Talbot, this unit will not only come into being, it will eventually be the best in the country. *And* the model that I want it to be.'

Annie, at first affronted by his quite accurate guess at her age, heard the fire of dedication in his voice. It made her study him more closely—the craggy face, with a straight sharp nose, firm

chin, untidy eyebrows over stern grey eyes—
and what she saw—and sensed in him—stirred
a feeling of true elation. Forget jolts of recognition and kisses in the past! If what he was
saying was true, then this was going to be the
job of her dreams, not just, as she'd thought
when she'd applied for it, a stepping stone to
something special. This was going to be the
something special she'd always hoped was out
there for her. The something special to which
she could dedicate her life!

Alex watched a whole array of expressions flash
across his companion's face. Used to reading
faces—how else could babies tell you how they
felt?—he saw puzzlement, then surprise, then
something that looked very like excitement.
Whatever it was, it brought a glow to her pale
skin, making the brush of freckles—a familiar
brush of freckles, he was sure—across her nose
and cheeks appear luminous. Then clear hazel
eyes lifted to meet his, and her smile lit up the
dreary lecture room.

'This, Dr Alex Attwood, is what I've been
waiting for for ever, it seems. Yes, I know about
hospital fighting and it won't only be hospital
against hospital, there'll be in-house battles as

well as other departments fighting to keep money or claim money they feel is being siphoned off to your unit.'

'Our unit,' he corrected, but he doubted she'd heard him, so intent was she on what lay ahead of both of them.

'But we'll fight and we'll win,' she continued, as if driven by some inner force. 'Because you're good—the best, most people say—at what you do, and because I'll be the best damn unit manager ever put on earth.'

She smiled at him again, triumph already shining in her eyes.

'You have no idea just how much this means to me,' she said. 'Thank you.'

Then, almost under her breath, he thought he heard her add, 'Again.'

Puzzled by the strength of her reaction, he forgot the puzzle of 'again' and considered where they stood. He was pleased to hear the commitment in her words and voice, but to be thanking him?

Did she not realise just how hard and dirty the fight ahead of them was likely to be? Didn't she realise she should be running for her life, not thanking him with such delight?

And why would any woman so obviously welcome the challenge the unit would provide? Most women he knew would back away—say thanks but, no, thanks.

Maybe she saw only the glory at the end— the image of herself as manager of an elite unit. But she looked far too sensible—and if she'd managed the PICU she was far too experienced—not to know how dirty hospital fights could get.

'To the best of our ability we'll ignore the politics,' she said—not 'we should' but 'we will'! 'We'll make our name on results. Of course, to get results you need the best staff, and that usually requires money, but if we have to work with what we have, then we've got to make them the best.'

'Hey, we haven't had the staff briefing yet, and already you're into staff training.'

She swung her head to look at him again, and the way her hair moved reminded him of moonlight on a lake, although her hair was dark and shiny, not pale as the silk he'd spun off silkworm cocoons when he was a child.

'Aren't you?' she challenged, and it took him a moment to think what they'd been talking about.

Of course he was. He'd thought of nothing else for weeks. Every free moment had been given over to working out how he could bring the unit staff to the level of expertise he'd require from them. But he wasn't sure he wanted to admit that to this woman just yet.

In fact, he felt a little put out—as if she'd taken some of his dream away from him, as if she was already sharing it.

Which was good, he reminded himself. The entire staff needed to share the dream—to be committed to it. And it wasn't that he wasn't ready to share, he just hadn't expected anyone to take it on board so wholeheartedly—so immediately.

Noises outside suggested other staff were arriving.

He glared at Phil as he wandered in, greeting Annie as if they'd been friends for years, putting his arm around her waist to draw her forward so he could introduce her to Maggie and Kurt and Rachel.

For one brief, irrational moment Alex was sorry he'd brought Phil to St James, then he remembered that Phil, for all his flirtatious ways and womanising, was one of the best surgeons

he'd ever worked with. He needed Phil here—
the unit needed him.

Besides, Annie Talbot had drawn away from
his arm, positioning herself out of touching distance of Phil.

CHAPTER THREE

'YOU'D like them, Henry. All of them. Even the boss,' Annie said, as they breakfasted the following day. 'Maggie's an Australian, from Melbourne, Kurt and Rachel are Americans—they came out to Melbourne with Alexander the Great.'

As Henry was the recipient of this information, she didn't have to explain that the title his staff had given him had stuck in her brain. That was the nice thing about talking to Henry. She didn't have to explain.

'Phil, although he's originally from England, came with them from the States as well, because he's learning under you know who for five years. Phil's a flirt with a predilection for blondes, I suspect. He's been chatting up Becky, the unit secretary, and she's blonde, and I saw him in the canteen with one of the unit nursing staff—another blonde.'

Annie reached up and pushed her hair back behind her ears, then she rubbed Henry's head.

'Good thing I've had a dye job, isn't it, Henry?'

But although she spoke lightly, her heart was heavy, and though the new job seemed to hold the promise that all her dreams could come true, she was edgy and apprehensive about working with 'the Great'.

She'd spent a restless night hovering in the no man's land between sleep and waking, trying desperately to rationalise this uneasiness, finally deciding that in part it was to do with her denial—that their work relationship had started off on the wrong foot because of that one word. Because of a lie!

But she couldn't have said yes—couldn't have admitted they'd met before then gone through the 'where and when' questions which would inevitably have followed. It was unlikely Alex even remembered dancing with a stranger one night five years ago, and to say 'I'm the woman you kissed on the terrace at Traders Rest' would have been too humiliating for words. Especially with Phil standing there, all ears.

And, she feared, it would have been too dangerous as well, for it would tie her to the congress, to the delegates—maybe even to Dennis…

Annie stood up, hoping physical movement would shake off the hungover feeling that was the legacy of her sleepless night. She patted the dog, called goodbye to her father and walked briskly out the door.

Today she wouldn't talk to herself, would look where she was going, would not bump into anyone and would not tell any lies. Even small ones. Even small self-protective ones.

'Good morning!'

Not Phil's cheerful cut-glass accent, but a slow, deep, American drawl. Alex was emerging from the front gate of the house four doors down.

'Good morning,' Annie managed, mentally noting that was lie number one and her resolution was already shot to pieces because there was nothing remotely good about having to walk to work with Alex.

'The meeting went well. The staff seemed enthused. You met with the nursing staff later— are you confident we'll have them all on side, even when things get tough?'

Annie should have felt relief that the walk to work was going to be nothing more than a business meeting with added exercise, but relief wasn't happening. What was happening was a hot flush. Premature menopause it must be, because just walking next to this man couldn't make her feel hot all over.

Very hot all over.

'Are you all right?'

Annie stopped walking and turned to glare at the questioner.

'Why wouldn't I be?' It *must* be early menopause—menopause made you snappy!

'You're a little flushed and you didn't hear my question.'

Alex Attwood was now frowning at her—so much for good mornings!—but it seemed more an enquiring kind of frown than an angry one, then he reached up and touched a finger to her cheek.

'You're not sickening for something?'

Only love.

The thought came from nowhere, and so horrified Annie she knew whatever colour had been in her cheeks was now gone as all the heat drained from her body, leaving her deadly cold.

'I might be,' she told him, 'and it might be catching.' She turned away to keep walking. *Think premature menopause, not love.* Although menopause itself wasn't contagious—and not really a sickness, either, though she was reasonably certain premature menopause could be classed as such. And as she'd now come up with a third symptom, fuzzy thinking—why else would love have popped into her head?—she was willing to believe that's what she had. Especially since she also had mood swings and she'd felt like crying when he'd touched her cheek.

'Annie!'

She'd been striding determinedly along the footpath, but something in the way he said her name made her look at him again. She read confusion on his face, yet he seemed to have nothing more to say.

Alex cursed his ineptitude with words. It had always been this way. As a child he'd made things with his hands, fixed things—found making a gift for his mother easier than saying he loved her.

Oh, he could talk about his work, to a certain extent. Though even there he preferred to do it—to operate—and to let the results do his talking.

But at some stage he had to talk to Annie, really talk to her. Find out if there was any validity in the way his thoughts kept imposing a fair-haired ghost over her features. Because if there wasn't, then he might be going mad. He might, as his sister had so kindly suggested when she'd visited him in Melbourne, be suffering the effects of living upside down for six months—mental muddle-headedness, she'd called it.

Though she'd only accused him of that because he'd refused to laugh at her absurd jokes and failed to accompany her on an umpteenth shopping expedition.

She'd walked on—Annie, not his sister—and had stopped at the lights on the busy intersection opposite the hospital. He took her arm as the green man indicated they should cross, and though he felt her soft muscle go tense she didn't pull away, accepting the touch as nothing more than a courtesy.

Not knowing that he'd *had* to touch her, *had* to feel her flesh and the hardness of bone beneath it. Closer to madness than mental muddle-headedness. He sent the thought-wave to his sister, now back in North Carolina with the rest of his family, then, the crossing safely negotiated, dropped Annie's arm and turned his thoughts to work.

'The staff are really keen. It was a good idea to negotiate to have our own staff treating our patients even once they leave the special care unit for the ward.'

'I'll be observing in Theatre Three today—adult patient but an intricate aorta repair.'

They spoke in unison, then Annie gave a laugh and said, 'As I was answering a question you asked ages ago, it seems only fair you continue.'

Though equally willing to talk about the nursing staff—anything to get his mind off the physical manifestations of Annie's close proximity—Alex continued.

'It was torn in a MVA, repaired at the time, but now the cardiologist feels there must be adhesions slowing the flow of blood through the vessel. The echo shows some kind of blockage but it's where the aorta's tucked away behind the pulmonary artery and it's hard to get a clear picture of the problem. Even the MRI doesn't show much.'

'Sounds tricky,' Annie said, though he guessed from the relaxation in her voice that she was relieved by the topic. 'I'm assuming that's this morning. You've a couple of patients booked for consultations this afternoon.'

They were inside the staff entrance, in the small alcove where he'd waited for them yesterday, and she turned and smiled at him.

'To think I doubted you'd get referrals. I know Phil laughed at me when I said as much yesterday, but I wondered if paediatric cardiologists here would prefer to continue to use the surgeons they knew.'

He found himself smiling back.

'I knew I could always take cases from the waiting list at Children's. That was part of the deal, but referrals? I had a few doubts about them myself,' he admitted, still smiling, because Annie's smile had brightened up his day.

He sent a new thought-wave to his sister. Total muddle-headedness!

Annie wondered if it was because they were in the hospital—on her home ground, so to speak—that she felt able to relax. Back there, when he'd said her name, even premature menopause couldn't explain away the quiver of excitement that had ricocheted through her body. But now they were talking work, and she was so relieved she smiled at him. A real smile, not a pretend one, so the score on small lies for the day remained at one.

And he was smiling back—which made her confidence on being on home ground waver slightly. But she held firm and asked about the operation, and somehow they made it to the office without any further manifestations of her condition.

Manifestations of something else, perhaps, when they'd bumped together in the lift, but it certainly wasn't love, she assured herself. Attraction, maybe. And why not? He was an attractive man.

That thought alone was enough to make her seek refuge in her work. It had been so long since she'd considered the attractiveness or otherwise of men, this time she felt a shiver, not a quiver, and the shiver was more fear than attraction.

'Come on, the unit can't afford too much overtime. We're all heading for that pub up the road for a drink to celebrate day two safely over.'

Phil had poked his head around the door and, looking at him, Annie suspected he hadn't poked more of his body into the office because the rest of it was attached to Becky.

'Maybe later. If you're still there.' Second small lie of the day as she had no intention of going near the pub. But it was only a self-preservation-type lie so surely that didn't count! 'Right now I have to finish some requisitions or the Great will have my hide.'

Phil rolled his eyes. 'Forty-eight hours into the job and he's got you bluffed already. Believe me, his bark is far worse than his bite—not that he barks all that often. Come and see the man relax—learn for yourself he's human.'

For some reason Annie's mind flashed to the kiss, and though she didn't tell Phil, she was willing to admit to herself that she knew for sure he was human.

'Maybe later,' she repeated, pulling a sheaf of paper across the desk to let him know she was serious about working.

He shrugged good-naturedly and walked away, but what seemed like only minutes later her diligence was again interrupted.

'Phil says you're not coming for a drink. He's blaming me—says I'm a slavedriver. Is there really so much work for you to do?'

Annie considered lie number three, then shook her head.

'Not really. I do want to check these letters going out to possible corporate sponsors. You mentioning that cardiac units can generate more money than most hospital divisions started me thinking. It won't take long, but I don't feel like going out tonight anyway. I've not let anyone know I'd be later than usual, so I'd prefer to go straight home.'

Was that a lie? *I'd prefer not to spend avoidable time with you* would be closer to the truth, but that could be translated into going straight home.

'There are people at home you have to let know?'

He asked the question softly, as if he didn't want it to sound like prying.

'Of course,' she said, answering the question yet knowing it wasn't an entire answer.

Knowing immediately from his silence he was waiting for the rest of it.

'Dad and Henry. Both at home. Waiting.'

The silence that followed this less than explicit explanation seemed to hover in the room like a third person, then Alex nodded briefly, said, 'Goodnight, then,' and walked away.

'If he'd asked, I'd have told him Henry was a dog,' Annie told the door which had closed behind him.

'Plege on!' Alex said, the order crisp.

Who outside this room could guess it meant

a cocktail of chemicals and nutrients, in the main a potassium solution—poison—would flow into the baby's heart?

The tiny heart stopped beating. It was pale and floppy-looking, clearly visible to Annie where she stood on a stool behind the heart-lung machine that was oxygenating the baby's blood while the intricate surgery took place.

She held her breath, knowing every second Baby Ross was on the machine increased the risk of long-term damage to his frail body. Alex had explained exactly what would happen at every stage of the operation. He'd called all unit staff, including the sisters from the special care unit, together and drawn diagrams on a white-board, but nothing had prepared Annie for how small and totally vulnerable Baby Ross would look on the operating table, or how desperately sad it would be to see the still, lifeless little heart.

She reminded herself his heart would start beating again within minutes. That Alex was the best at what he did. She swallowed the lump of fear for Baby Ross that had lodged in her throat, and concentrated on what was happening now.

The switch, they called it. Baby Ross had been born with TGA, or transposition of the great arteries, which in effect meant that oxygen-rich blood from his lungs, instead of being pumped around his body, was being pumped back into his lungs, while oxygen-depleted blood was recirculated through the rest of his body.

Baby Ross was unlucky to be born with TGA, but his lucky break had been being born in St James's—Jimmie's as the staff called it—not just at any time but three days after Alex and his team had begun work there.

Annie studied the man they called 'the Great'.

Cool. Detached.

Ruthless?

She wasn't sure about the last, although both the other words would describe her impressions of the man. Having worked with critically ill children for the last five years of her career, Annie knew both the children and their parents needed very special characteristics from their doctors and nurses—characteristics like warmth, compassion, understanding.

Yet the parents she'd seen with Alex in consultations in his rooms didn't seem bothered by his attitude. In fact, some of them—the fathers in particular—seemed to appreciate the forth-right way he described their child's condition, and the deliberate way he warned them that all surgery had potential dangers for the patient, who could die or be brain damaged for life.

The first time Alex had said this in Annie's hearing, she was sure she'd reeled from the shock, but in retrospect had decided it was only fair the parents knew the risk, although Alex had quickly followed up his warning with statistics proving how unlikely such an outcome was.

Her thoughts were wandering but her eyes followed every move of the surgeons' hands. Alex, Phil and a surgical registrar Annie didn't know were all working on this one small mortal, while Rachel passed instruments and Kurt Reynolds operated the heart-lung machine, making sure the flow of blood was just right for tiny fragile arteries and veins. Maggie Walsh gave blood-gas readings and oxygen perfusion rates in a calm, relaxed voice.

Maggie, a petite brunette, oozed confidence, a great asset in an operating theatre where things could so easily go wrong. Even when Baby Ross had arrested earlier, she'd remained calm, giving Alex the information he'd needed, easing everyone's tension with her quiet calls of pressure and blood gas.

Was she involved with Alex?

Annie wasn't sure why the thought entered her head, but once it lodged there she looked from Maggie to Alex, considering the idea. Almost wishing she'd gone to drinks with them on Tuesday evening so she could have seen them together socially.

She gave an impatient shake of her head and turned her attention to the tiny form on the table, although she was sure she felt a frown gathering on her forehead and there was a definite squeamishness in her stomach.

Nonsense!

She concentrated on the operation, watching the glove-sheathed fingers of the surgeon sew with thread so fine she couldn't see it. The clock on the heart-lung machine ticked off the seconds. Baby Ross had already been dependent on it for over an hour. Below the clock, another set of digital numbers—the baby's core temperature. Baby Ross's blood had been slowly cooled as it had gone through the machine so when the machine was stopped for the final stages of repair, he wouldn't suffer brain or other organ damage.

All this Annie knew in theory—theory she'd brushed up on before the hour the staff had spent in front of the whiteboard—but her own heart thudded with tension as the operation continued. How much could this tiny baby take?

She looked at Alex again, and saw the precision with which he moved, the teamwork between himself, Phil and Rachel. They made it look easy—a symphony of hands moving in concert—and though one small slip could mean the baby died, Annie couldn't feel any tension emanating from the group.

A little of her own tension eased, as if their confidence was transferring itself to her, but when the heart was stimulated and cannulae to and from the heart-lung machine were removed, the tension built again, until the little heart pumped on its own and the repairs to the big vessels held.

A faint cheer from Phil, while Alex nodded his satisfaction, stepping back from the table and pausing there while the circulating nurse unplugged his light.

Annie glanced at the clock and saw the operation must have proceeded according to plan, for Alex's estimation of the time of completion of the major work had been spot-on.

He would now leave Phil and the registrar to close.

Annie remained where she was. She hadn't done much theatre work in recent years, but she knew from her work in paediatric special care units that every stage of an operation was important. OK, if Phil slipped up and didn't insert his stitches into Baby Ross's chest just so, it might not make a difference to the final outcome of the operation, but regularly spaced stitches put equal pressure on the fine new skin, so the wound healed more quickly and left less scarring.

She gave a nod of satisfaction as she saw Phil's work. He might be a light-hearted flirt outside the theatre, but in here he was as meticulous as his boss.

Alex, still trailing the cord from his light, stripped off his gloves and gown and dumped them in a bin. The design of the new theatre meant all the electrical equipment was contained in one central column so there was no tripping over leads and having no room to move because of bulky equipment. Even the echocardiogram machine was fitted into the column, with screens around the walls of the theatre so everyone could see what the machine found.

In this case, as Kurt, who was working it, had run the sensor over Baby Ross's chest, it had showed blood flowing sweetly through the switched vessels, and now the camera in the column was focussed on Phil's hands as he closed.

Alex sighed, awed as ever by the insults such small mortals could take to their bodies and yet survive. Behind him, an increase in the chat level signalled the operation was nearly at an end. Normally, he'd be operating again within an hour, but he'd deliberately not scheduled anything for this week, wanting to get the unit organised to his satisfaction first. Baby Ross had been an emergency admission—and in some ways it was good to get that first op out of the way.

Annie had said as much when he'd called the staff together for a pre-op briefing, and he'd wondered if she'd been as nervous as he had been about this first case in the new unit.

Annie, or Rowena?

He shook his head, unable to figure out why he couldn't let it go. OK, so he'd looked for his ghost on and off for years, trawling through the names at medical conventions, checking lists of hospital employees. Not all the time—not obsessively—not *quite* obsessively…

She didn't give much away—the woman everyone knew as Annie Talbot. Very self-contained. Very cool. Utterly charming to everyone she met, yet detached somehow.

He smiled to himself—knowing that was exactly how people described him. But he had his reasons for avoiding emotional involvement. Although he rarely admitted it, his job made huge demands on his emotions. To hold the life of a newborn infant in your hands—to hold the dreams of the infant's parents—this was where his emotion was spent.

So where did Annie spend hers?

On Henry?

Was he a boyfriend? Lover? Partner?

He turned as he remembered she was here in the theatre. Remembered telling her he wanted her to observe the operation. She was still perched on the stool, and he saw her give a nod as if approving Phil's handiwork.

'Can I help you down?' he said, then clutched at her waist as she wobbled precariously.

'Sorry, you startled me,' she said, her soft throaty voice made huskier by the mask she was wearing, although she was beyond the vital 'clean zone' of the theatre. 'Yes, I could do with a hand to get down.'

Eyes he'd thought green earlier today but which now seemed blue looked down into his then slid away as if embarrassed by his closeness, while beneath his hands he could feel her body contracting—drawing away from his touch.

Drawing away as it had once before...

What rot! his brain scoffed as he lifted her easily and set her down on her feet. But the speed with which she stepped back made him wonder if it had been rot, or if she had indeed flinched from his impersonal touch.

Not that it mattered one way or the other. Now she'd seen something of his work, there'd be no further need for her to be lifted off the stool by himself or anyone else.

Especially not Phil, who'd taken the liberty of lifting her up there!

'That was unbelievable,' she said. 'I'm glad you suggested I watch.'

She'd moved to the wall and was watching the screen that showed the registrar, under Phil's instructions, securing the drains, catheters and pacemaker wires on the baby's body.

'That's the pacemaker,' Alex explained as she peered closer to see Phil adjust the wires. 'It's there in case Baby Ross's heartbeats need regulating over the next few days. A heart that's suffered the trauma that one did during the op might not work perfectly as it heals. We give dopamine as well, to keep it beating.'

Alex saw Annie nod at his explanation but her eyes remained on the screen as she watched the final stages of the operation. She lifted her hands to untie her mask, undoing the top strings and letting it dangle, revealing a slight smile hovering on her pale, curved lips.

'You must have done so many, to be so sure in all your actions.'

The words, and possibly the smile, were meant for him, but her eyes, and, he thought, her attention were still on the screen.

'What now?'

'For Baby Ross?' Alex said, coming closer so he could check the tubes and wires were all positioned as he liked them. 'He'll go back to the PICU on the respirator, and we'll see how he is when he wakes up tomorrow. Sometimes babies are strong enough to breathe on their own after twenty-four hours, but this little chap was so young, we'll just have to wait and see.'

He paused then touched her lightly on the shoulder.

'Good to have the first one over?'

'I was thinking that myself,' she said, 'though it seems unfair to be pleased about something when that little fellow has been through so much—and will go through more before he can be discharged.'

'We should always be pleased when things go right,' Alex told her. 'Things go wrong all too often, so it's right to rejoice in successes.'

She studied him for a moment, then nodded and smiled.

'OK, I'll rejoice without the guilt,' she said, and walked out of the theatre.

Alex followed, pausing at a cupboard outside the theatre to pack his loupe into its special wooden case, then he did the same with the fibre-optic light. Tools of his trade, he thought, as he often did. More important for the delicate and intricate work he did than the needles and thread. Well, maybe not more important, but as important. Weird conversation to be having with himself, but a successful operation invariably left everyone on a high, and his high, since he'd lifted Annie off the stool—felt his fingers span her tiny waistline—seemed to be taking off in an unexpectedly sexual direction, so it was better to think about loupes and lights.

At least she'd walked away now, so his physical awareness of her had lessened.

Was it because she reminded him of the ghost that he felt this?

Because she might be the woman who'd featured, on and off, in his dreams for the last five years?

He shook the thoughts away.

It wasn't that he was against involvement with work colleagues, although personally he did his best to avoid it, but Annie gave off vibes that would put off any but the most determined of suitors. There wasn't much of her—above medium height but slim, almost willowy, yet she generated an enormous amount of 'don't mess with me' attitude. Even Phil had backed off his usual flirtatious approach.

Though knowing Phil, he was probably planning to come at her from a different angle. Alex caught his finger in the catch on the box and cursed softly. At least he told himself it was the catch that had made him swear.

Why Phil felt that every pretty woman he met presented him with a challenge, Alex didn't know. Though to be fair to Phil, he usually went for blondes so maybe Annie would be safe from his attentions.

She'd better be, he grumbled to himself as he changed, but the possibility that Phil might consider a darker-haired woman as fair game rumbled within him as he made his way to the office.

Annie looked up from some paperwork as he walked in.

'I saw Baby Ross's parents on my way here,' she said, 'and told them everything had gone well. I said you'd probably see them in the special care unit later. Coffee and sandwiches should be here any minute.'

Alex's scraggly brows drew together in a frown.

Had she come on too strong? Made herself sound too businesslike?

Should she not have spoken to the Rosses?

She was about to apologise when the frown cleared and he smiled. At least, she thought it was a smile. It wasn't exactly radiating warmth and sunshine, but it stretched his lips and even pressed the hint of a dimple into his left cheek. Something she hadn't noticed before.

'I'm sorry, I was still thinking about the procedure.'

His excuse sounded lame, but Annie could hardly accuse him of lying to her about his frown. As if it mattered, she scolded herself crossly, watching him settle his rangy frame into the comfortable chair on the other side of her desk, then reach for the sheaf of mail she had waiting for him.

But somewhere deep inside her was a niggling feeling that it did matter. She could tell herself it was because this new work relationship was the most important one in her career thus far. That this was her dream job, and she wanted to get it right from the very beginning. But she didn't think she'd believe it...

An aide came in with a tray holding a big pot of coffee—Annie was getting used to Alex's coffee addiction now—two mugs and a plate of sandwiches. She lifted the plastic wrap off the sandwiches and pushed the plate towards him, then poured his coffee, glad to have something to do while her mind teased at the niggle she was feeling.

OK, so there were some small hitches. The long shadow thrown from the past for a start, but if she kept denying they'd met before—not that he'd ever mentioned it again—surely they'd get past that.

And then her attraction to him—she'd get past that as well.

And as long as she was here and Dennis was in the US, then any tenuous link between him and Alex wouldn't matter.

Maybe—eventually—when Alex went back to the States, it would be different. Maybe then there'd be some danger. Maybe, just before he left, she'd have to tell the truth…

Satisfied with this decision, she reached out for a sandwich, mistiming the movement so her hand brushed his. He looked up from the letter he was perusing, the movement so quick she knew he'd felt the same jolt she'd experienced. More electrical than sexual, like a mild shock.

'Dry air?' His eyebrows lifted and his lips half smiled as he asked the question, but Annie, mesmerised by that half-smile, couldn't answer. She looked away, while heat again surged into her cheeks.

'It must be,' she said, released from the spell and using her hands to hide her colour. Then, after checking his hands were nowhere near the sandwiches, she reached out again.

Alex tried to concentrate on the letter he was reading, but knew he'd have to read it again later. In another room. Away from Annie and the strange effect she was having on him.

He glanced at her, head bent as she ate her sandwich, pretending to be reading the file in front of her. He knew she was pretending, because he was as well. Silky dark hair fell forward on either side of her face so all he saw was the curve of her cheek, pale as cream, enhanced rather than marred by that light scattering of freckles bridging her neat, straight nose.

A slim, neat, self-contained person, he guessed, but super-efficient, according to Col Bennett, the CEO.

He remembered the way his hands had almost spanned her waist and the feeling of lightness as he'd lifted her off the stool. Remembered the same feeling of lightness as he'd danced with his ghost. Was he still in post-op euphoria that he couldn't concentrate on business matters? That he was distracted by this woman?

Post-op euphoria was common, although, generally speaking, he didn't get it after a straightforward operation like Baby Ross's. Different hospital, new theatre—either could explain it. But did the euphoria usually take the form of distraction?

Not women-type distraction, he was sure.

In fact, a lot of his ability to focus so strongly on the job stemmed from his deliberate decision to avoid women-type distraction. Not avoiding women as such, just any distraction associated with them.

Avoiding emotional dependency.

The woman he was pretty sure wasn't distracting him gave a little cough and he realised he'd been miles away, lost in his thoughts—distracted!—instead of checking his mail and giving her answers to any questions she'd written on it.

'What if I take it all through to my office and rough out some answers for you?' he suggested.

'No way,' she said, then, perhaps noticing his surprise, she added, 'I've worked with doctors for years. That mail will go into your office and not be seen again for months. No, Dr Attwood, today's the day. There's nothing difficult, and if we work through it together we should be finished by the time you've eaten your lunch.'

'Slavedriver,' he muttered at her, and heard her laugh.

The sound, so clear and fresh and light-hearted, startled him, and he looked across at her again and decided maybe he was wrong about her being his ghost. His ghost had had dark, bruised shadows under her eyes, and had carried a weight of sadness he had felt as he'd danced with her.

Annie Talbot of the carefree laugh was exactly who she said she was, a super-efficient, career-driven woman who would help him make his dream a reality.

She leaned forward again, jotting a note on the file, and he saw a line of pale hair along her parting. The sight jolted him nearly as much as her touch had earlier. She was either prematurely grey, or dyed her blonde hair dark. And didn't women usually go the other way—go blonder rather than darker?

CHAPTER FOUR

ANNIE heard the hum and beep of the machines that guarded Baby Ross's life, but they were no more than background noise, a kind of counterpoint to her thoughts. It was late evening, but she'd been unable to go home without seeing him again, and now she was sitting by his bed, her forefinger gently stroking his skin, and wondering about fate.

A sound outside, beyond the glass, made her look up. How appropriate—here was fate himself.

The door opened, and Alex walked in.

'He's doing well—better than I'd expected,' he said, and Annie nodded.

'I know. I'm not here because I'm worried, but because Madeleine—Mrs Ross—needed to sleep and she wasn't happy about leaving him on his own.'

Alex smiled.

'Then you'll be pleased to know the cavalry's arrived. I've just been talking to Ben, Madeleine's husband. He's come down from the

71

country with a tribe of relatives—a brace of grandparents, several aunts and the odd cousin, if I got the introductions right.'

'I'm glad they're here,' Annie told him, ignoring the squelchy feeling of regret she'd felt as Alex had spoken of family. She, too, had a brace of grandparents, several aunts and various cousins—relatives she no longer saw, who no longer knew where she was, or even who she was. 'Madeleine's been strong, but she's still only, what, three days post-partum, and she needs to look after herself as well. With family support she should be able to do that.'

The door opened again and Madeleine Ross returned, with a tall, suntanned man she introduced as Ben. As she moved to the bed to introduce her husband to their son, Annie slipped away.

She assumed Alex had stayed to answer any questions Ben might have, so was startled when he joined her in the lift.

'Are you heading home?' he asked, no doubt finding the conclusion easy as she had her handbag slung across her shoulder.

She nodded confirmation and edged slightly away, although there wasn't much room for manoeuvring in a lift crammed with end-of-visiting-hours commuters.

'I'll walk you there,' he announced, leaving no room for manoeuvre at all.

She could hardly say there was no need when he lived only four doors up the road, and they could hardly make the walk—if he was going to his place—ignoring each other.

So they left the building and walked through the soft autumn night, cutting down the side street away from the hospital traffic and along the tree-lined avenue where they both lived.

'I flew up a month ago to look for a place to rent then I saw these old houses and knew I wanted one,' Alex remarked. 'They're like something out of a fairytale.'

They were. It was exactly what Annie had loved about them, but walking with Alex in the lamplit darkness had filled her with too much emotion for speech so she made do with a nod of agreement.

Until they passed his house.

'You've missed your gate,' she told him, stopping on the pavement outside his place. He smiled at her.

'I'm walking you home, remember?'

'It's only four doors. I hardly need an escort.'

'No, but I'll escort you anyway,' he said, and waited patiently until she began walking again. 'See you safely home to Henry and your father.'

Already confused—by the walk, his presence, her own reactions to it—she was even more fazed by his mention of the dog. Suddenly letting him believe Henry was a person seemed unfair and yet...

Surely it was OK if she was doing it for protection?

Protecting herself against herself?

They reached her gate and he leaned over to open it. A low, gruff bark woke the night's stillness, and as Alex straightened he smiled.

'Henry?'

Then, without acknowledging her reluctant nod of agreement, he put his hand behind her back and guided her down the path, up onto the little porch with its gingerbread decorations and into the shadows cast by the huge camellia bush that grew beside the fence.

And Annie went, propelled by something beyond the pressure of his hand on her back. Guided by the acceptance of fate.

He turned her, slid his hands behind her back and drew her close, then he bent his head and kissed her.

Annie stood there, held not by the light clasp of his hands on her back but by memories, then, as the gentle, questing exploration continued, she kissed him back, losing herself in sensations she'd forgotten existed because five years ago she'd been too frightened to enjoy them.

The kiss went on for ever—nothing hasty or half-hearted in Alex Attwood's kisses—but just when Annie knew her knees were going to give way beneath the emotional onslaught, he raised his head and looked into her eyes. Another long moment, then he said, 'I had to know!' And walked away.

Annie slumped against the wall and watched him. Up the path, out of the gate, along the street, in through his gate—then he disappeared behind the shrubbery in his front yard.

Thoughts and feelings battered at her, so strongly felt she rubbed her arms as if to stop them bruising. Clearest of all was the knowledge that Alex knew exactly who she was—maybe not her old name, but certainly that she was the woman on the terrace.

Annie was certain of this because, although she'd have scoffed if someone had suggested to her that all kisses were different, she'd certainly have recognised Alex by that kiss.

So, he'd left the ball in her court. It was up to her to admit they'd met before, or to carry on the charade. Thank heaven it was Friday and she had two whole days before she had to see him again.

Before she had to sort out the muddle in her mind...

'I know I don't *have* to go to work, Henry, and I know going up there carries a risk of running into Alex, but it's early—barely six-thirty—and not many people will be out of bed, and I want to see for myself how Baby Ross is doing. Maybe they've even decided on a name for him. I'll just slip up there, then come back and take you for a walk.'

Lacking a waggable tail, Henry made do with wiggling his hindquarters on the floor at the sound of his favourite word, but he obviously hadn't taken much notice of the first part of the conversation because the moment Annie stood up, he fetched his lead and stood hopefully beside her.

'Put it down before it goes all mushy,' she told him, then added, 'Later,' knowing it was one word he did understand. Food, walk, later, fetch—he had quite a vocabulary.

She walked to the hospital, adding words to her list of Henry's vocabulary, deliberately not peering towards the front of the house where Phil and Alex resided.

Fancy buying a house when you were only here for twelve months! Although houses in this area were a good investment...

Thinking about the house was better than thinking about the man, or thinking about the situation the two of them were now in, so she mused on why someone might buy a house for a short-term stay all the way to the hospital and up to the fourth floor.

'I'm sure he's more alert than he was,' Madeleine Ross greeted her when she walked into the room.

The sister on duty had reported a quiet night, and assured Annie all the monitor results were positive.

'It was weird, working in here on my own and with only one baby,' she'd added. 'Though staff from the special care unit next door, your old stamping ground, kept popping in to see me.'

'Make the most of the quiet time,' Annie warned her. 'You know how hectic it can get, and I have a feeling that will happen sooner rather than later.'

'Once word gets out Dr Attwood is operating here, you mean?'

Annie nodded. She'd had her doubts but referrals were coming thick and fast, from as far afield as Indonesia and the Middle East.

She sat with Madeleine until Ben returned with coffee and a doughnut for their breakfast, and was about to leave when Ben asked her to stay.

'We want to ask you something,' he said. 'About the baby, but not about his health. About his name.'

Annie waited.

'It's like this,' he said, so slowly she wondered if he was having trouble finding even simple words. 'We had names picked out, but now they don't seem right…' There was a long pause, then Ben looked at his wife as if he didn't know how to continue.

Annie came to his rescue.

'They were names for a healthy baby—a different baby you'd pictured in your mind.'

She smiled at both of them, and touched her hand to Madeleine's shoulder.

'It's OK to feel that way. In fact, it's healthy to grieve for that baby you didn't have. It's natural for you to have a sense of loss.'

'It's not that I don't love him,' Madeleine hastened to assure her, touching the still arm of the little mortal on the bed.

'I know that,' Annie said. 'Of course you do. You probably love him more because he needs so much help. But you can change your mind about his name—call him something different.'

'We'd like to call him Alexander, after Dr Attwood,' Madeleine said shyly, and Annie smiled, wondering how many little tots with congenital heart disease were trotting around America, proudly bearing the same name.

'I'm sure he'd be honoured,' she said, and heard a voice say, 'Who'd be honoured, and by what?'

He was there again—as if she was able to conjure him up just thinking or talking of him. Like a genie in a bottle. Not a good thing when most of the genie-in-a-bottle stories she'd heard had terrible endings!

'I'll let Madeleine tell you,' Annie said, and she slipped away.

It had been stupid to come up here. She'd *needed* two whole days—two months? Two years?—to work out how to tackle the recognition thing. *And* the kiss! Now here he was, back within touching distance again. Or he had been until she'd fled the room.

Determined to head straight home and thus avoid any chance of having to walk with him, she was leaving the ward when the sister called to her. A different sister, seven o'clock change of shifts having taken place while she was in Baby Ross's room.

'We've a new admission coming in. Sixteen-month-old baby, Amy Carter, shunt put in to deliver blood to her lungs at birth, but now something's gone wrong. Dr Attwood's called in all the theatre staff. He's briefing them in half an hour.'

The information upset Annie. She should have been the first one called so she could contact the necessary staff. She'd been at home until half an hour ago. She had her pager.

She touched her hand to her hip and realised she didn't have it! How could she have been so careless?

She didn't like to think about the answer to that, because she knew it involved distraction, and the reason for the distraction was so close.

But she was here now—she could be in-volved.

Alex came out of Baby Ross's room—Alexander's room?—at that moment and she turned to him, ready to confess her mistake, but he did little more than nod at her before entering the next room where, Annie guessed, Amy Carter would be nursed.

Annie followed him, and saw him peering at the X-rays in the light cabinet on the wall.

'You've heard we've an urgent referral on the way?'

He didn't wait for an answer, but pointed to a small tube clearly visible in the cloudy murk of the X-ray.

'The cardiologist sent these on ahead. I be-lieve in shunts—I use them myself in a lot of cases. You can insert them through a thoracot-omy, rather than cracking open the chest, which is far less traumatic for the infant, and by putting in a shunt you give the baby time to grow, and give the heart muscle time to firm up so it's not like sewing mousse.'

He had his finger on the shunt, as if he could feel the small plastic tube itself rather than the image of it.

'The other school of thought, of course, is to do all the repairs as early as possible—do a switch like we did on Baby Ross within days of discovering the problem. That saves the baby another operation later, and is possibly easier on the parents in the long run, but to me it's still a huge insult to a newborn infant and the softness of the tissues can lead to complications. Stitches not holding, that kind of thing.'

He was frowning as he spoke, voicing a debate that must often rage in his head, but when he'd switched off the light he turned and smiled at Annie.

'I'm operating in an hour. As you're here, do you want to watch? I didn't call or page you because I felt you deserved a day off, and you've seen one switch. This will be similar.'

'I'd like to watch.' Mental apology to Henry—did he understand 'later' was a very indefinite concept?

'Good.'

Alex walked away, leaving Annie wondering just where things stood between them. This was *not* the post-second-kiss conversation she'd expected to have. Had he forgotten what he'd said last night?

Or did he have no wish to pursue it—now he knew she'd lied to him?

Or—duh!—maybe he was just better than she was at separating work from personal matters.

Whatever, it didn't matter. Alex was working and she was here to see it all went smoothly. Theatre first.

Rachel was supervising the scrub nurse setting out what the surgeons would need, telling the nurse, a lanky six-footer called Ned, what would be happening.

'I saw him at work in an adult cardiac operation the other day,' Rachel said, following Annie out of the theatre. 'I think he's good and I'd like to think we can keep him.'

'If you want him, he's yours,' Annie promised her. If he was equally popular with the adult cardiac surgeons she might have a battle, but she was willing to fight for whatever they needed to make the unit work. She was good friends with the director of nursing and would speak to her first thing Monday.

'Saturday morning—I was going sailing on the harbour with some mates from the UK, and what happens? The slavedriver drags us all into work.'

When Annie went in, Phil was sitting in the office, drinking a cup of coffee from the machine she'd had installed to feed Alex's habit. She smiled at Phil's grumble, made a note about phoning the DON, then asked who else was coming.

'Not Maggie. She had the good sense to get out of town for the weekend. Alex has got some hospital anaesthetist—with paediatric experience—so we should be OK.'

'And Kurt?'

'Yes, he'll be here. As a matter of fact, I think Kurt sleeps with his machine, and as it's now fitted in Theatre here, he was probably asleep beside it when the call came.'

Phil was still grumbling when they moved to the little lecture room, where Alex had already drawn a diagram of Amy Carter's heart on the whiteboard. With simple words, and an economy of description, he outlined what he intended doing, pointed to the spots where trouble could be expected then asked for questions.

'I saw the X-rays,' Phil said, surprising Annie, who thought he'd been mooching in her office since his arrival. 'There seemed to be a lot of scarring on the heart—far more than there should be if the duct was inserted through a thoracotomy.'

Alex sighed.

'You're right. I looked at it with Annie, and hoped I was wrong, but I've just received another file—fortunately, her parents had kept a comprehensive one as they moved from hospital to hospital. She's had two operations already. The first tube became compromised and they opened up her chest. We're going to be going through a lot of scar tissue, both outside and inside.'

'So we don't really know what we'll find in there,' the registrar suggested, and Alex agreed.

'Expect the worst in these situations,' he said, 'then if things aren't as bad, you're pleasantly surprised.'

'And if it is the worst?' Ned asked.

'You have to remember that this little girl will die without the operation,' Alex said carefully. 'She may still die with it. I've just told her parents that. She could die on the table and we might not be able to save her. But we go into every operation confident of a positive outcome. If I didn't feel that way, I wouldn't do it.'

This operation was different. Annie felt it in the tension that vibrated around the room, and heard it in the quiet swear words Alex and Phil were both muttering into their masks.

She could see for herself the difference between Alexander Ross's heart and the scarred, gristly organ little Amy was carrying inside her chest.

Alex, no doubt conscious of the registrar and his need to learn and understand, explained things as he went—explained what should be happening, and how little Amy's tiny heart should be configured, cursing only when he found too many anomalies.

'The problem is the heart has compensated for its weakness. The coronary arteries, feeding blood to the heart muscle, were compromised when the shunt was put in, so the body has grown new vessels and now we've this bizarre network and can't be sure what we can safely touch.'

He bent his head to his work again, then added, 'Touch none of them is the rule in these cases. If you don't know what it is, don't touch it.'

Four hours later Alex thanked them all and left the theatre. Ned helped Annie down from her stool, and she followed Alex out, passing him as he packed away his loupe and light just outside the door.

'Annie!'

She stopped and turned towards him. The equipment he'd been wearing had left parts of his face reddened and his cheeks were drawn. He looked exhausted.

'Are you doing anything now?'

'Right now? Going to my office.'

'After that—are you busy?'

He paused and rubbed at the red marks on his face as if they bothered him.

'I know you have a life, and you have no obligations to me, but...' Another hesitation, then he said, 'I don't know the area. I have to shop or Phil and I will starve to death over the weekend. I need a guide to help me get my bearings.'

Annie's turn to hesitate.

It wasn't much to ask, but it would put her in his company for the rest of the day.

'I've promised Henry a walk,' she said, and saw Alex smile.

'But that's great. Minnie needs a walk as well, and though I've seen the park down the road, I don't know where dogs can or can't go. We'll walk them both and then we'll shop, grab some lunch somewhere along the way. I'll change, see Amy's parents, then collect you from the office and we can go home together.'

Go home together! The three words rang in Annie's ears, prompting a surge of loneliness.

But she wasn't going to be seduced by words or loneliness. This was a business proposition. They'd walk their dogs—presuming Minnie was a dog—then shop, and that was it.

'I'm worried about that baby.'

Alex's opening remark as they left the office reassured Annie. The business side of things had been confirmed.

'She's been through so much,' he continued, putting his hand behind Annie's back to steer her into the lift. 'And she was really down when she came in. Can a child in such a debilitated state survive another major operation?'

'But you must have seen so many children like Amy. There must be plenty of cases where you've been called in after a previous operation hasn't worked.'

He nodded, and escorted her out of the lift.

'Of course, but I still worry every time. It's one of the reasons I'd like to see more trained paediatric cardiac surgeries, and units set up specifically to handle congenital heart disease. CHD is the most common of all congenital conditions and the long-term survival rate of children who have surgery is excellent. It's not a question of allocating blame in an operation that's gone wrong. I understand the difficulties a cardiac surgeon who operates on adults ninety-nine per cent of the time must face when he sees a neonatal heart. But it needn't happen—he wouldn't be forced to operate—if there was a paediatric cardiac surgeon within reach.'

'But would that have made a difference to Amy? Having someone more skilled to do the op?'

They were outside the hospital now, walking towards the crossing, and Alex paused and looked down at Annie.

'Are you really interested or just making conversation?' His voice made a demand of the question and she frowned at him.

'Of course I'm interested. What are you thinking? That I'm asking questions so I'll *sound* interested in your job? That it's a way of showing interest in you? As if!' Scorn poured like hot oil over the words. 'I'd like to remind you that it's my unit, too, but I can't run it effectively if I don't know as much as I possibly can about it.'

Alex saw her anger reflected in her eyes, and wondered how an intelligent man like himself could always find the wrong thing to say to a woman.

But walking with Annie—talking about work—had made him feel great—comfortable, relaxed and at ease with the world. Then his pessimism had surfaced, and with it memories of women who'd shown interest in his work early on in a relationship, then had blamed his job for the breakdown of the same relationship.

Not that this was a relationship. Other than purely work-related...

Not yet, hope suggested.

Maybe not ever, pessimism reminded him, giving an extra nudge with a reminder that she'd lied about not having met him before.

Unless she really didn't remember...

Damn his pessimism! Right now he had to make amends to his colleague.

'I'm sorry. I don't know why I said that. Of course you're interested.'

They resumed their walk, but he'd lost the conversation. It was being with Annie that was the problem—being with his ghost. The kiss, if it had done nothing else, had confirmed that.

But it *had* done something else. It had stirred his blood and not a little lust, so he'd walked home determined to get to know her better. Actually, he'd walked home with phrases like 'woo her and win her' running through his mind, but in the sober light of day he had modified these aims.

In the sober light of day he'd also found his tattered list of the delegates at the congress, and had gone through it once again, searching among delegates and partners for an Anne, or Annie, even Joanna and Annabel—any name that might conceivably be shortened to Annie.

He hadn't found one, and couldn't help but wonder just who she was.

Get to know her first, he'd decided, yet now here he was, treating a simple question with suspicion.

'So, are you going to answer me, or shall we continue this walk in silence?'

'What was the question?'

'I asked about Amy. Would it have made a difference if she'd had a paediatric cardiac surgeon do the first two ops?'

Alex set aside thoughts of stirred blood and lust and concentrated on his reply.

'I couldn't say that. So much can go wrong. There are risks involved in all operations. But I firmly believe we can cut down on the percentage of risks with more specialists and specialist units.'

They'd reached his gate and Annie stopped.

'I want a shower, and need time to write a shopping list if we're shopping straight after we drop off the dogs. Say half an hour? You'll be going past my gate to get to the park so I'll wait for you there.'

'*You'll* wait for me?' he teased, eager to rebuild the relaxed atmosphere they'd shared early in the walk.

'Yes, I'll wait for you. I don't subscribe to the ''women are always late'' theory. I find, in fact, that women are more likely to be on time than men.'

She walked away from him, leaving him wondering just where things stood between them.

Not relaxed and easy, that was for sure! Her pert retort had underscored that point.

CHAPTER FIVE

ANNIE managed to stay angry with Alex until she saw him emerge from his front gate twenty-five minutes later. Though it wasn't Alex emerging from the gate that made her laugh, but the little black bundle of curls trailing along behind him on the end of a lead.

Alex Attwood had a *spoodle*! A designer-bred spaniel-poodle cross, clearly still a puppy as it was the size of a large guineapig. The little thing cavorted along behind him like a curly black wig caught up on a rat on speed.

'I hope you're not laughing at my dog,' Alex said, though the corners of his mouth were twitching as if he understood her mirth. 'And you know the old joke about a little dog killing a big dog. Tell your Henry he'll choke to death if he tries to swallow Minnie.'

But Annie didn't have to tell Henry anything. He was sitting at her feet, forty kilograms of Rottweiler muscle and bone, gazing at the little poodle with love-struck eyes, while she yipped and yapped about his feet, and explored him as if he were a new kind of doggie toy.

'She's gorgeous,' Annie said, kneeling down to pat the excitable little creature. She covered Henry's ears with her hands and added, 'I fell in love with these dogs at the pet shop, but really needed something big and fierce.'

Loyalty made her add, 'Not that Henry's all that fierce, it's just his size that frightens people.'

'I can see he's not that fierce,' Alex said gravely, and she looked down to see Henry was now lying down, so the little dog could lick his face and climb across his back.

'He's supposed to frighten people, not other dogs,' Annie said defensively, then realised this conversation was veering dangerously close to places she did not want to go, so she called to Henry and started walking towards the park.

'There's a dog-walker who walks Henry and other dogs in this area every weekday,' she told Alex, pleased they had the dogs to talk about. 'Mayarma, her name is. If Minnie stays inside while you're at work, you'd have to leave a key. She collects Henry and his lead from my dad, but other dogs she picks up straight from the yard. Are you interested?'

'Very,' Alex told her. 'If someone could walk Minnie during the week, I wouldn't feel guilty about not walking her at weekends, and as perfect strangers react to seeing me walking her as you did—with hysterical laughter—I'd as soon skip the park sessions. At least with you beside me, people might assume she's yours and we've just swapped leads.'

Annie listened to the grumble but guessed he was far too self-assured to care what other people thought about his dog. But the conversation did raise a question.

'If you're embarrassed walking a wig on legs, why buy a spoodle?' she asked.

'Buy a spoodle? Do you seriously think a man my height would buy a dog this size? That I wouldn't have considered the aesthetics of the situation?'

'A girlfriend's dog?' Annie guessed, although the idea of a girlfriend brought a stab of jealousy in its train.

'My sister's idea of an ideal companion for me,' Alex told her, gloom deepening his voice. 'My sister has despaired of me ever having a long-term relationship with a woman, so when she was visiting me in Melbourne a month or so ago she bought me the most curly, frilly, impossible sort of dog she could find. To keep me in touch with my feminine side, would you believe?'

Annie was laughing so hard she had to stop walking, although Henry, determined to stay close to his new friend, was dragging on his lead.

'She *is* all woman,' she conceded. 'That's if dogs can be classed that way. Look at how she's vamping Henry.'

They were entering the park, and as dogs were allowed off their leads in this part of it, she bent to unclip Henry's.

'Will she come when you call?'

Alex looked at his small responsibility.

'Who knows?' he said. 'She's been to puppy school, but seemed to think it was a place she went to flirt and play with other dogs. How seriously she took the lessons I don't know, because sometimes she'll obey all the commands she knows, but at others she's totally deaf.'

'Maybe Henry will teach her some sense,' Annie suggested, although the way he was behaving made her wonder.

But Alex unclipped Minnie's lead anyway, and the two dogs, so absurd together, gambolled across the grass, Henry using his huge paws with gentle insistence to guide the smaller dog around the trees and bushes.

'I usually sit over there,' Annie said, pointing to a comfortable seat beneath a shady tree. Since meeting Minnie and laughing at Alex's story of her advent into his life, she'd relaxed. He'd made no move that could be indicative that she was anything other than a colleague, so she could put the kiss down to him wanting to prove something to himself.

Or to both of them.

And from now on, colleagues were all they'd be, so when he said things like 'walk home together' and she felt prickles of excitement, or when he put his hand on her back to guide her into a lift and she felt tremors of attraction, she had to pretend it hadn't happened, and act like the efficient, dedicated, focussed unit manager he wanted her to be.

It's what you want to be as well, she reminded herself.

Alex could feel the woman's presence on the bench beside him—feel it like a magnet drawing him towards her. But he didn't move.

He thought instead about the conversation they'd had earlier—about one snippet of it. About her needing a dog that was big and fierce.

Because she was a woman living alone?

But she wasn't—her father lived with her.

He remembered the bruised shadows under her eyes, the vulnerability he'd sensed in her five years ago. He thought about her change of name, and anger coiled like a waking serpent in his gut.

No, he was letting his imagination run away with him. There could be any number of reasons for a woman to change her name. Marriage was the obvious one. Attractive woman—she could easily have been separated and married and separated again in five years.

He glanced towards her, doubting that scenario. It didn't fit with the sensible woman he was coming to know—a sensible woman now smiling at the antics of the dogs, then laughing as Henry toppled Minnie with his paw, then rolled around on the grass so the little dog could climb all over him.

Once again Alex heard the joy and light-heartedness in the sound and saw a glimpse of the warm and vibrant woman inside her efficient, work-focussed façade. But she'd laughed earlier, when he'd told her about Minnie coming into his life, then she'd shut that woman away and become a colleague again, as if that was all she wanted to be to him.

Yet last night, when he'd kissed her, there'd been more. He was sure of that. As sure of it as he was that she was his ghost.

As sure of it as he was that he wanted to know more of Annie Talbot.

As sure of it as he was that he wanted to kiss her again.

'Are you doing anything tonight? Hot date?'

His thoughts must have prompted his subconscious to ask the question because it was out before he'd had time to think it through. Or consider how Annie might react to it.

She turned towards him, and studied his face for a moment, a slight frown replacing the smile in her lovely eyes.

'Why do you ask?'

He shrugged—tried to make less of the question than there was.

'I thought as we're shopping, I might get the ingredients for a curry. I do a mean curry but it's hardly worth making it for one person and, knowing Phil, he won't be home on a Saturday night.'

'You're asking me to have dinner with you tonight?'

She spoke the words carefully, as if she needed to make sure there was no misunderstanding.

He answered just as carefully.

'Yes.'

A long silence, until Alex realised he was holding his breath. He let it out as silently as he could—a sigh might have made him sound impatient.

'I don't date,' she said at last, which wasn't an answer but was ambiguous enough to give him hope.

'It needn't be a date,' he told her. 'Just a couple of colleagues sharing a meal.'

She studied his face again, as if trying to read his thoughts behind the words, and her frown deepened.

Then *she* sighed.

'I don't know, Alex,' she said softly. 'I don't think it's such a good idea.'

He sensed her backing off—felt her retreat—and moved to stop it.

'Sharing a curry? What harm can come of that?'

Another pause, so long this time he *had* to breathe.

Then she said, almost to herself, 'Who knows?' and shrugged her shoulders.

There was something so pathetic in the words—so vulnerable in the gesture—it took all the restraint Alex could muster not to pull her into his arms and promise to protect her from whatever it was she feared. Because fear was certainly there. It was in her eyes, and in the quietly spoken words.

In the big fierce dog.

And still she hadn't answered.

She looked away and whistled to her dog, and as he came gambolling back towards her, Minnie herded in front of him, she straightened her back, squared her shoulders and turned to smile at Alex.

'Oh, what the hell!' she said. 'Yes, I'd like to share a curry with you, Dr Attwood!'

Henry brought Minnie safely to their feet, received a pat and a 'good dog' from his mistress, then as she clipped on his lead and stood up, she said to Alex, 'They were once herding dogs, you know, Rottweilers. They followed the Roman armies across Europe, herding the animals they kept for meat. Apparently some instinct still remains in Henry.'

Alex heard the words. He was even interested in the content. What he couldn't follow was the switch in the woman who was now walking on ahead of him, back towards their respective houses. Had she reverted to this 'unit manager' persona so he wouldn't be under any misapprehension that their dinner together tonight was in any way a date?

He didn't know, but he did know that the more he got to know Annie Talbot, the less he really knew of her!

Anxious about Amy's condition, they called at the hospital before hitting the mall. The little girl was stable—which was as much as Alex felt he could expect at this stage. After talking to her parents for a while, he climbed back into Annie's car, a big, comfortable SUV, and they drove the short distance to the shops. As he had been in Melbourne, Alex was surprised by how familiar the mall seemed, although Annie called it a shopping centre.

He was also surprised at how many things *he* considered staples went into Annie's shopping trolley. The same brand of pancake mix he used at home, pretzels, sourdough bread and even tart green pickles.

Well, since last night he'd known she was the woman on the terrace, so she'd been in the US then. If she *was* Rowena Drake—or had been in the past—then she'd lived over there for some years. He knew enough of Dennis Drake's history to know that—even knew he'd been married when he'd first arrive to work in St Louis.

But a number of her purchases were unusual. OK, the amount of dog food was explained by Henry's size, but so many cans of soda and packets of crisps?

'My dad's a writer—he says munching helps him think,' she said, as they pushed their trolleys towards the checkout.

'A writer? What does he write?'

She smiled at him.

'Mysteries. Detective stories. They've only just started being published in North America so even if you read mysteries, you probably haven't heard of him.'

'I do read them—all the time. They're my relaxation. What name does he write under?'

A beat of excitement in his heart. Would he learn Annie's maiden name if her father wrote under it?

Would that help him get to know more about her?

Probably not.

He realised he'd missed her answer, and blamed it on untangling his trolley from the woman in the queue beside him.

'Sorry—what name? His own?'

'Yes. Rod Talbot,' Annie said, and Alex felt relief.

So she'd left Drake for whatever reason and had reverted to her own name. And her real first name could well be Rowena, with Annie a family nickname, and she'd reverted to that as well.

And he'd had her with serial marriages!

Then the name she'd said sparked recognition in his brain.

'But I've read his books! Or some of them. They're set right here in Sydney, aren't they? A friend, knowing I was coming here, lent me a couple, then while I was in Melbourne I tracked down a few more.'

He was genuinely excited, having enjoyed the fast, racy read Rod Talbot provided. And to think he was Annie's father!

She was unpacking her trolley onto the checkout counter at this stage and he wondered if he should ask her father to dinner as well. There was obviously no Mrs Talbot in the picture, and if this *was* just a neighbourly, colleague type dinner, then asking her father would be the right thing to do.

But in some uncharted territory of his heart, he was aware that this wasn't just a neighbourly dinner—or a colleague-with-colleague one. He wasn't sure what it was, maybe a first small step towards something, but, whatever, he wasn't going to invite a third party to partake of his curry. Not tonight.

Annie, refusing his offer of help to unload her groceries from the car, dropped Alex and his shopping off at his front gate, then drove around the block and down the lane behind the row of houses, into the garage behind her house.

She turned off the engine, opened the door but didn't get out. Instead, she slumped across the steering wheel in relief. Shopping with Alex had been far too intimate an experience for her to ever want to repeat it.

'Intimate?' she muttered to herself, as the thought registered in her brain. 'Shopping?'

But she couldn't find another word for the confusion of symptoms she'd displayed as they'd pushed their respective trolleys up and down the aisles. No premature menopause this time, for which, she supposed, she should be grateful.

But empathy, togetherness, bonding stuff had happened, and when they'd both reached for Aunt Jemima's pancake mix at the same time, and they'd turned towards each other and laughed, a heap of other emotions had fluttered in her heart. Emotions she didn't want to think about.

'It was pancake mix, for Pete's sake,' she said to Henry, who'd come out to the garage to see why she was so slow at bringing in his food supplies. 'You can't get all squishy and romantic over pancake mix. Especially when the other pancake-mix purchaser would have been considering his stomach, not his heart.'

Henry gave her his 'don't take it out on me' look and sat, willing, if necessary, to wait by the open car door for ever.

'I'm coming,' Annie told him, reaching over the back of the seat to pick up her first load of supplies. 'At least now he knows where the shops are, so there'll be no excuse for the two of us to ever shop together again.'

She hauled the bags out and started towards the house, arms getting longer by the second as innumerable cans of dog food weighed them down.

'Which reminds me, Henry. That dog of Alex's eats about one hundredth of what you do. Shopping would have been a lot easier if I'd got a spoodle.'

Henry was unperturbed by her rant, even helping out by nudging the back door open for her.

But Henry was no help at all as she dressed for a curry dinner with a colleague. Her black jeans were fine, but what top? The T-shirt with a pattern and a few sequins to make it sparkle wasn't dressy but might be considered so for a casual dinner, yet a plain T looked *too* plain, and her white shirt looked like work, while the green one—a favourite—had developed a nasty habit of popping the top button, revealing too much cleavage for a curry with the boss.

'If he hadn't been with me, I could have ducked into that new shop at the mall,' she grumbled at Henry, who was watching her fling tops on and off with a tolerant expression on his face.

In the end she settled on the white shirt, but tied a lacy, emerald green scarf around her neck.

'Life's all about compromise,' she told the dog. 'And, no, you weren't invited. Which is just as well because if Minnie saw you drooling near a dinner table she'd go right off you.'

Her father was out, so she said goodbye to Henry and walked up the road, with each step regretting her decision a little more.

It wasn't that she didn't want to see Alex, or try his curry, just that the thought of an evening alone with him—any time alone with him—filled her with a cocktail of contradictory emotions.

So she was enormously relieved when it was Phil, not Alex, who opened the door to her.

'I never disturb the chef when he's creating,' he told her, welcoming her with a huge smile and an only slightly less huge hug. 'Come on in. See our place. Is it very different to yours?'

Annie looked around. It was furnished very differently—a man's abode—but the house plan was the same and a sense of familiarity made her feel instantly at home.

Phil was explaining how his date had stood him up, and was ushering Annie in, arm around her waist, when Minnie came hurtling from the kitchen to greet the new arrival.

Annie scooped up the little dog, using the movement to move away a little from Phil. She held the black bundle of delight close to her chest and pressed kisses on its soft, curly head, then glanced up to see Alex watching from the kitchen door.

Watching and frowning.

'What? I'm not allowed to kiss her? But she's adorable!'

The frown disappeared, replaced by a smile.

'Kiss away,' he said easily, but Annie had to wonder what he'd been thinking to prompt the frown. 'Phil's told you he's joining us?'

Annie nodded, still cuddling the dog.

'I did offer to go out rather than play gooseberry,' Phil said. 'But Alex assured me it was only a neighbourly, colleague type dinner and I didn't feel so bad.'

Annie had been thinking of saying much the same thing to him—hadn't she spent the short walk convincing herself that was all it was?—yet she felt put out that Alex had been so quick to label it that way.

That's all it is, she reminded herself as she set Minnie back on the floor, but as she straightened she saw Alex give a little shrug, and wondered if he'd felt the same disappointment.

'You might offer our guest a drink,' Alex said, then he disappeared back into the kitchen.

'Is he the kind of chef who hates having an audience as he works, or could we join him in the kitchen?' Annie said, holding the light beer Phil had poured her. 'It seems kind of antisocial to be drinking out here while he's slaving in the kitchen.'

'I wouldn't venture in there,' Phil said. 'You've heard him swear when things go wrong in Theatre. Well, he's twice as bad in the kitchen.'

But if you weren't here, surely I'd have been invited to join him, Annie thought, but she didn't say it, wondering if Alex had regretted his decision to ask her to dinner and persuaded Phil to stay.

Then Alex announced the meal was ready, and Phil escorted Annie into the big kitchen where the table was set with an array of condiments and sambals, and the tantalising scent of curry spices filled the air.

'After living with him in Melbourne, I know the deal with the little dishes. These are all cooling ones,' Phil said, pointing to cucumber in yoghurt, and sliced fruits, 'while the chutneys will make it hotter. Don't touch this one, potent chilli, unless you like eating fire.'

Annie glanced at Alex, wondering if he minded Phil taking over the host's role, and saw the real host smile, sharing her amusement at Phil's behaviour.

'I don't mind a bit of fire,' Annie said as Alex sat down and put a little of the chilli on the side of his plate.

Again Alex smiled at her, and a warmth that had nothing to do with curry, or the chilli sambal, or even premature menopause, spread through her.

Forgetting to feel apprehensive about whatever was happening between herself and Alex, she relaxed, settling down to enjoy the food and the conversation, pleased to be sharing talk and laughter with these two men.

The phone rang as they were finishing their second helpings, and Alex, who was closest to the kitchen extension, reached out to answer it.

He was on his feet within seconds, assuring someone he'd be right there.

'It's Amy. Her temperature's going up and her blood count down—could be a haemorrhage somewhere.'

'I'll go,' Phil offered, but Alex shook his head.

'No, it's my job to see it through. Let Annie finish dinner and you see her home. You can come up then if I'm not back.'

Phil's behaviour was exemplary, and when he put his arm around her as they walked back to her place, she accepted it, knowing he was a toucher, and telling herself they'd be working together for a year and she'd better get used to it. But having Phil walk her home wasn't the same as having Alex do the short trip, and she felt a surge of regret that he'd been called away.

A totally uncalled-for surge of regret, given how adamant she'd been about their dinner together not being a date.

Phil saw her safely to her door, said goodnight, took a couple of steps towards the gate, then turned.

'I'm sorry it was Alex called away, not me,' he said. 'He doesn't do much relaxing and I think an evening with you would have been just what the doctor ordered for him.'

He grinned at her, then added, 'Just what this doctor would have ordered, anyway.'

He hesitated, as if expecting her to say something, and when she didn't, he spoke again.

'Are you interested? In Alex?'

Another pause during which he maybe realised he'd overstepped some invisible boundary.

'Not that it's any of my business,' he added quickly. 'But I kind of like the chap and I'd like to see him happy. Not that he's not happy. Lives for his work. But that's hardly a balanced life.'

Annie beat down the excitement this conversation had generated, and said quietly but firmly, 'I don't think we should be discussing Alex behind his back.'

Phil seemed surprised, but he took it well, shrugging his shoulders and repeating his goodnight. Then he walked off up the road, not turning in at his gate but going on to the hospital.

Where little Amy was fighting for her life!

Annie wanted to call Phil—tell him she'd go with him—but there was nothing she could do up there, and Amy was in the best possible hands.

But knowing that didn't help her sleep, and at five she gave up, got out of bed, showered and dressed and walked up to the hospital.

The first person she saw in the ward was Alex. An exhausted, unshaven-looking Alex, who greeted her with a tired smile.

'You know, you're admin staff now and don't have to be here all the time,' he teased, and she was pleased to hear the words, certain he wouldn't be making light-hearted comments if Amy hadn't survived the night.

'She's all right?' Annie asked, needing the verbal confirmation.

'She's one tough little lady,' Alex said. 'It's an infection, not a haemorrhage—thank heaven.'

Then he rubbed his hands across his face.

'Fancy thanking heaven for an infection in so frail a child, but I doubt she'd have survived another operation. We've done a culture and now have gram specific antibiotics running into her, and she's slowly improving. I'm worried about fluid retention. The kidneys are susceptible to damage when a patient's on bypass, and I hate to think we've added kidney problems to her other burdens.'

'Catheter OK?' Annie asked, remembering a child she'd nursed who'd had every test imaginable for bladder and kidney problems, and in the end the trouble had been with his catheter.

'I like your thinking,' Alex told her. 'They're such tiny tubes for infants, they could easily block or kink. I'll check that now.'

Annie stayed and talked to Amy's father, who came out of the room while Alex watched the intensivist on duty remove the old bladder catheter and insert a new one.

'He's been here all night,' Mr Carter told her, nodding towards the glass-enclosed room where they could see Alex bending over the bed. 'I doubt my wife would have gone away to have a rest if he hadn't persuaded her *and* promised he'd stay himself until she got back. You don't get many specialists like that.'

'No, you don't,' Annie agreed, feeling ashamed she'd regretted him being called away, though it had hardly been a date with Phil there. Then she wondered just when Mrs Carter *would* get back. Alex, too, needed to sleep.

Annie went into the next room, where small Alexander Ross was now off the ventilator. An older woman—one of the brace of grandparents, no doubt—was dozing in the chair beside his bed.

'He's doing well enough to be going to the ward tomorrow.'

Annie swung towards the speaker, and then regretted it, because she wanted nothing more than to run her hands across his face, smoothing away the lines of tiredness.

'That's wonderful,' she said instead. 'His recovery's going far better than we'd expected, isn't it?'

Alex nodded then led her out of the room.

'Far better,' he confirmed. 'Are you going back home now you've checked on your two patients?'

'I suppose so,' Annie said, 'though Dad will still be in bed so I thought I might stop at the canteen for breakfast. They do a wicked big breakfast here.'

'I obviously didn't feed you enough last night,' Alex said mournfully. 'But now you mention it, a big breakfast might just hit the spot. Mrs Carter is back with Amy so, come, let me escort you to the canteen.'

He bent his arm and held it towards her and Annie could hardly refuse to tuck her hand into the crook of his elbow. What did surprise her, though, was the way Alex then drew her hand close to her body and, in so doing, drew her body close to his.

'Story of my life,' he said conversationally as they walked along the corridor to the far lift that would take them directly down to the canteen. 'Phil and I entertaining a beautiful lady, and he gets to take her home.'

He was holding her too firmly for Annie to pull away, and she hoped he didn't feel the blush that spread through her body.

'Beautiful lady, indeed!' she scoffed, as they reached the foyer and were waiting for the lift. 'Look at me! Straight out of bed into jeans and trainers—slept-in hair and no make-up.'

But if he heard the last part he gave no sign of it, saying only, 'I do look at you, Annie,' in a voice that made her toes curl in the tips of the maligned trainers. 'All the time.'

CHAPTER SIX

'WHAT do you mean?'

Her voice seemed to come from a long way off, and it wavered slightly, but she got the question asked.

Alex looked down at her and a smile shifted the lines in his tired face.

'Just that,' he said. 'I find myself looking at you—or looking for you if you're not around. Part of it's to do with a ghost who's haunted me for the past five years, but more to do with the flesh-and-blood woman who came into my life less than a week ago. Crazy, isn't it?'

The lift arrived and they squeezed in, Alex still holding her close. The lift was full of staff heading for breakfast, and various acquaintances greeted Annie. Hospital gossip being what it was, she was glad she was working in the unit now and not out on a ward where she'd have been teased unmercifully about such blatant behaviour as standing arm in arm with her boss.

But the press of bodies also saved her answering Alex—had she had an answer—and they travelled in silence, then discussed food options as they stood in the queue, everything so back to normal that Annie thought they were safely past the conversation until, once seated at a table in a quiet corner of the room, Alex reintroduced it.

'You must think I'm crazy, and maybe I am. If this conversation embarrasses you, please write it off as lack of sleep, but yesterday in the park I spent so much time assuring you that dinner would just be a colleague-with-colleague thing—emphasising the casualness of it—and then I had to leave you with Phil last night. Phil with his charm and his good looks and his success with women! I was caught up with Amy and there you were with Phil—that's when I realised.'

He stopped, perhaps realising now that he wasn't making a lot of sense, and looked across the table at Annie. Then he shook his head, and this time his smile was tiredly rueful.

'What I'm trying to say in my inadequate way is that I like you, Annie Talbot. I'm attracted to you, and if it's OK with you, I'd like to get to know you better.'

Excitement vied with apprehension, but beneath both these emotions was a longing so deep Annie was shaken by it.

It was a longing for love in the biggest, widest, most wonderful sense of the word. A longing to be part of a couple—to share a little of another person's life, to give and take support, to have someone to laugh and cry and rejoice with, to have someone to hug, or to give a hug to when a hug was needed.

'What really rocks me is that I thought I'd got over wanting someone in my life,' she said, looking at Alex as she spoke, knowing he probably wouldn't understand, as she was no better with words than he had been. 'I've built my life as a single person and, truly, Alex, I've enjoyed it. I *do* enjoy it. I have company when I need it, a job I love, I'm career-focussed and happy that way.'

Alex watched her carefully choosing words and putting them together. He listened to them and though they didn't spell it out, he was reasonably certain she was telling him she was no longer quite as happy with her chosen path, which, as far as he was concerned, was tantamount to admitting she was as attracted to him as he was to her.

'Eat your breakfast before it gets totally cold,' he told her, though he smiled so she would know it wasn't an order.

She smiled back and a little of his tiredness lifted. Somehow they'd muddled through a very awkward conversation and reached a place where he was pretty sure they could go forward.

Together.

On a kind of trial basis.

He felt an insane urge to shout or clap or otherwise celebrate this breakthrough in the Annie-Alex relationship, but then he remembered other relationships he'd had and the dismal hash he'd made of them. He watched Annie cut a piece of bacon then spear it on her fork, and more doubts assailed him.

Not doubts about Annie and wanting to get to know her better, but doubts about his ability to make her happy—to chase away the shadows he sometimes saw in her eyes.

Was he, with his antipathy to and avoidance of emotional dependency, the right kind of a man for Annie? Could he give her the kind of unconditional love she would need to heal whatever wounds she carried from the past? And wouldn't wrapping Annie in the kind of love she needed mean unwrapping the protective barriers he'd erected around himself? How else could he bring her close?

And had she actually said she was happy to get to know him better? No, she hadn't. She'd waffled on as badly as he had, and hadn't really said anything at all when you got right down to it.

Because she wasn't sure?

Wasn't sure about exposing herself to love and perhaps to whatever hurt it had brought to her before?

So he'd have to be mighty careful! Mighty sure that nothing he did would put her in more emotional jeopardy.

'Aren't you going to eat yours?' she asked, drawing his wandering thoughts back to the here and now.

'I'd better, hadn't I?' he said. 'Or I won't have the strength to walk you home.'

He watched her as he spoke and saw the shadows he'd been thinking of chase across her face, and he felt a steely resolve to do whatever he could to chase those shadows away.

'It's not commitment, Annie,' he said quickly, not wanting to lose her before the relationship had begun. 'Just a ''getting to know you'' kind of relationship. A ''let's see where it goes'' experiment.'

The shadows cleared and she smiled at him.

'In the interests of science, of course,' she teased, and Alex felt the tension drain out of his body. Yes!

He didn't punch the air, not physically, but in his head he saw his fingers clench and his hand go up in triumph.

Because she'd tentatively agreed to get to know him better?

Come on, man!

But he couldn't curb his inner excitement, though he hoped it wasn't showing on the outside.

He attacked his breakfast, barely noticing it was less appetising than it would have been if eaten hot, but before he'd finished his pessimism had surfaced again, reminding him he was a stranger in a foreign land, in a city he didn't know. Where was he going to take Annie for a first date? First dates should be special.

'What are you worrying about now?' she asked, reminding him he had company at the table.

'How do you know I'm worrying?'

'Your eyebrows knit together.' She softened the blow with another smile. 'And your lips go tight.'

He tried loosening his tight lips with an only slightly tight smile, and admitted his dilemma.

'I don't know where to take you. For our first date.'

He'd expected understanding, but not laughter. She laughed and laughed, the sound so joyous he couldn't help but enjoy it, though he was a little disgruntled that he could cause such mirth.

'It's not a cardiac operation,' she said when she'd controlled herself enough to speak. 'It doesn't have to be planned to the nth degree. We can go to the beach—or for a walk around the harbour foreshore. We can eat at the Thai restaurant down the road from where we live, or at the little Italian place on the other side of the park.'

And why are you suggesting places to go with this man when you know full well you shouldn't be seeing him at all? Annie's head asked her, but the longing had won out over caution, and already she was excited about going to the beach or walking the foreshore with Alex.

If he ever had any time off, she amended as a buzzing sound had them both reaching for their pagers.

'It's mine,' he said, pushing back his chair and standing up. 'It's the ward. I'll phone from over there...' He nodded towards the house phone on the wall. 'But if it's the unit, I'll have to go.'

He hesitated for a fraction of a second, then reached out and touched his hand to her hair.

'May I call and see you later? When I've slept and showered and shaved?'

Big moment this, but Annie barely hesitated.

'I'd like that,' she said, then she looked up into his face. 'But if you don't make it, I'll understand. You need to catch up on your sleep. That's far more important than visiting me.'

Alex smiled at her.

'I wouldn't be too sure about that,' he said, then he lifted a strand of hair and gave a gentle tug. 'See you later, Annie Talbot!'

Annie Talbot! If only she *was* Annie Talbot! Annie Talbot could certainly have a 'getting to know you' relationship with Alex. Or run with a 'see where it goes' experiment.

After all, the man was returning to the US in a year. It wouldn't be a for ever and ever kind of relationship.

She worried about it all the way home.

'So, what do you think, Dad?'

Her father was breakfasting with Henry in the kitchen, and as he had so willingly gone into exile with her—had, in fact, arranged a lot of it—she'd had to share this new development with him.

'You like him?'

'I do,' she admitted, then she took a deep breath. 'But there's more to it than liking and more complications than a quick romance with a nice man. Remember I told you about dancing with the man on the terrace at the hotel? The night I left Dennis? The night I phoned home?'

'I remember too much about that night,' her father growled. 'Too bloody much!'

Annie reached out and squeezed his shoulder.

'It's all behind us, Dad,' she said. 'We've moved on. Anyway, he's the man. Alex is. He's the man I danced with that night.'

'Then I should like to shake his hand,' her father said, not seeing the point Annie was trying to make.

'You will, and maybe soon, but you won't say anything. That's the problem, Dad. Don't you see? He moves in the same circles as Dennis. You've done so much to hide me from him and his private investigators, and by getting close to Alex I could wreck all that.'

'If he's a decent man, there's no way he'd betray you to that—that animal!'

'He *is* a decent man, and that's what worries me. I'll be going into a relationship with him, however casual, under false pretences—knowing it can never go anywhere, that I could never marry him. Oh, I know I'm looking too far ahead, and we might never get that far in our relationship, but if we do…'

She broke off, unable to put into words the uncertainty she felt.

'What if you enjoy the present and let the future take care of itself, love?' her father suggested, covering her hand with his and giving her fingers a squeeze. 'You had precious little happiness in your life with Dennis, for all your insistence he wasn't always the way he turned out. You deserve all the love that comes your way. Go for it, and we'll sort out what needs to be sorted out when and if it happens.'

Annie felt her heart lift at her father's assurance, though some doubts remained. Plenty of doubts!

Alex was as good as his word, arriving early evening, freshly showered and shaven and slightly less tired-looking, wearing black jeans and a charcoal polo shirt and looking so—so manly that Annie felt her heart skip with excitement, the way it had when she'd been a teenager on one of her very first dates.

'You'd better come in and meet the author,' Annie suggested, when they'd both stood awkwardly on the doorstep for far too long.

'I'd like that,' Alex replied, and Annie relaxed. For a moment there she'd thought it was all going to fall apart—her with her skipping heart, dry mouth and brain that refused to function, and Alex thinking who knew what about the dummy who'd opened the door.

Primed to say nothing about the past, Rod Talbot greeted Alex easily, but Annie knew his sharp eyes were taking in the man, and his writer's mind would store all the conversation for perusal later.

'Annie tells me you've read some of my books. I hope they haven't had you cursing over the author's ineptitude.'

'On the contrary,' Alex said. 'I've found them good fast reads. Totally engrossing. And though I don't as yet know Sydney, you paint a picture of a fascinating city.'

'It is that!' Rod said, and Annie smiled to herself, remembering the hours she and her father had spent exploring the city when he'd first decided to set his mysteries here.

She watched Alex as he chatted to her father, bringing up scenes from the books he'd read, asking questions about writing.

'Can you type or do you use a voice-activated programme on a computer?'

Her father held up his hands.

'Tactful way to ask the question,' he answered. 'Rheumatoid arthritis—terrible disease. Started out thinking I'd save my hands—had knuckle replacements and all, but no good came of them. No, the voice programme works for me. You have to train them, you know, to your own voice and words, but Katy—I call mine Katy—makes me feel as if I've got a secretary. Katy knows me nearly as well as Annie does.'

'Dad also runs a tape recorder, so if something happens to the computer version of the story, he's got it on tape.'

'But what about changing things—going back over to take something out or put something in? I have to do that all the time just writing a paper, so that must be hard.'

'I have a real secretary for that,' Rod explained. 'She comes for three hours every afternoon and we tidy things up. I can type a bit so I do some of that part as well.'

'And you're fairly mobile? Able to transfer yourself? Do you drive?'

Annie smiled to herself. She'd heard Alex ask the parents of his patients personal questions that seemed unrelated to their child's condition, but knew he liked a whole picture of the family, saying it helped him see what stresses might arise later when they were responsible for caring for their convalescing child.

Her father seemed untroubled by Alex's interest, explaining he could take care of himself, just used the chair for mobility because his hip joints made walking both painful and risky. But, yes, he drove—had a lift on the car to put his wheelchair on the top of it, and used hand controls fixed to the steering wheel.

'It's the very latest system. Would you like to see it?'

'I would,' Alex said, and Annie started planning dinner. Her father was enjoying Alex's company and Annie knew Alex was genuinely interested, not just trying to make a good first impression. In fact, she doubted it would occur to Alex that he *was* making a good impression.

'We may as well eat here,' she said, when they returned an hour later—her father having taken Alex for a drive to show him how the car worked.

Alex began to protest, but Annie shook her head.

'We can go for a walk after dinner,' she told him. 'After all, you cooked for me last night— why shouldn't I cook for you?'

Henry, who'd greeted Alex earlier, sniffed around him, looking for Minnie, and not finding her had gone to bed, now heard the magic word 'walk' and appeared from the laundry where he slept.

'Not you,' Annie told him.

'Best you take the dog,' her father said, but Annie ignored the comment, instead instructing the men to sit down and asking Alex what he'd like to drink.

'Dad and I will both have red wine. Would you like a glass or would you prefer something else?'

'A glass of red would be great,' he said, and went on to mention some of the Australian red wines that had become his favourites.

'Lucky you,' Annie told him, showing him the bottle before she poured. It was on the top of his list!

'So we've similar tastes in red wine at least,' he said, smiling at her, though with a rueful look in his eyes as if to apologise about this 'first date'.

But the evening, for Annie, was just perfect. Alex seemed right at home, discussing books and wine and making them laugh at the things he'd found hard to understand when he'd first arrived in Australia.

'Just because we speak the same language, we assume we understand each other,' Annie said, about to recount an anecdote about her early days in the US then remembering she shouldn't. She changed the conversation to pronunciation differences, talking about New Zealanders and South Africans rather than Americans, but she guessed Alex had caught the conversational shift.

It was impossible, she decided. She couldn't go out with Alex, not if it meant pretending she'd never lived in the US. Not if it meant never acknowledging she was the woman he'd danced with on the terrace. How could they ever be at ease if that knowledge lay unspoken between them, yet how could she explain—tell him about that night—without telling him more?

She looked at him, his craggy face alive with intelligence and good humour as he explained the intricacies of American football to her father. Everything she knew of Alex indicated he was a good man—firm and demanding of his staff but quick to praise their efforts. Honest in his dealings with his patients' parents, yet empathetic as well, so they trusted their children's lives to him and knew he'd do his best.

But he wouldn't tolerate sloppy work, or anyone doing less than their best. She also knew, instinctively, he wouldn't tolerate deception, and what else would a relationship between them be?

She cleared away the dishes while Alex drew a diagram of a football field in the notebook her father always carried, and talked about offensive plays and touchdowns. By the time her father had learnt all he needed to know to enjoy the

American football games he watched on cable television, Annie had stacked the dishwasher and put a plate of cheese, fruit and biscuits on the table.

'No more food!' Alex protested. 'In fact, I think it's time I walked off some of that delicious dinner.'

He turned to Annie.

'You mentioned the beach, and I know it's not far away. Shall we go there for our walk? I'm happy to drive if you direct me.'

Annie hesitated.

'You go,' her father said, no doubt aware of all the machinations of her mind.

Annie nodded, thinking the beach would be as good a place as any to tell Alex what she had to tell him. To tell him she didn't think even a getting-to-know-each-other relationship would work.

'I'll just get a jacket. I can duck up the back lane and meet you at your car,' she said, but Alex shook his head.

'I'll wait for you. We'll go together. We'll sneak away without our respective dogs knowing what we're up to.'

Annie slipped upstairs, heart again skipping with excitement although she kept telling it this was the end, not the beginning.

Alex drove easily, and in one of life's little miracles they found a parking space not far from the wide concrete steps that led down to the beach. It was after eleven and only a few people wandered along the broad strip of sand, although a scattering of couples and groups, drawn to the soothing sounds of the surf, were walking on the promenade.

Annie breathed deeply, drawing the damp, salt-laden air into her lungs.

'I love standing by the Pacific and thinking the next big lump of land it hits is America. I love the idea that the water in a wave I'm watching here might one day, depending on the currents, wash across a beach in California.'

Alex put his arm around her shoulders and pulled her body closer to his.

'Should we talk about the big lump of land that is America? About North America in particular?'

Annie sighed.

'We should, Alex,' she said, relishing his warmth and closeness, wishing with all her heart this could be a real 'first date' so they were coming together with nothing but expectations of fun and pleasure—with no baggage from the past. 'But I'm not sure that I can. Or ought to…'

She couldn't go on, couldn't come right out and say, *I'm living a lie*.

'Then we'll walk,' he said, his voice strained. 'But one day, Annie, I hope you'll feel you can trust me well enough to talk.'

His disappointment in her was so obvious, it cut into Annie like a scalpel.

'Maybe we shouldn't even walk,' she muttered, but Alex was already guiding her towards the smooth wet sand where the waves finished their journey across the Pacific. He released her for a moment to slip off his shoes and turn up the bottoms of his jeans, and she bent and took off her sandals. Then, with his arm around her shoulders once again, they paddled through the shallows to where the beach ended in a high tumble of rocks that stretched, like the humped back of some fossilised sea creature out into the waves.

And in the shadow of the rocks he turned her towards him and drew her body close to his, then bent his head and kissed her with a mastery his previous kisses had ensured.

Annie was surprised at how familiar his body felt, how at home she felt in his arms. And the kiss. It was a different kind of magic—sweet, gentle and seductively addictive.

Until the first easy exploratory moves were done! Then the attraction she felt for Alex fired a need so deep and filled with longing she couldn't pretend, even to herself, that this was just a casual, first-date kind of kiss. This was a kiss that sent tendrils of desire spreading through her body, seeking out the deep-hidden places and bringing nerves and flesh to life with a tingling, trembling, pleading anticipation.

Somewhere there was noise. Loud noise. Annie hoped it wasn't her making it—whooping and crying out as her body delighted in Alex's embrace. Then Alex gently put her from him.

'Someone's in trouble,' he said, sounding as breathless as she felt. At that moment Annie saw the source of the noise, a young man standing on one of the humps of rock, calling for help.

'Someone swept off the rocks,' she guessed. 'Fishermen usually.'

They were both scrabbling towards the lad who was still yelling for help but not offering any more information until Alex reached him.

'It's Dad. He slipped and backwash carried him out. I can see him in the surf but I can't reach him.'

Other beach-walkers were gathering on the sand at the base of the rocks.

'I've called triple O,' one said.

'My wife's run back to the lifesavers' club-house. There's usually someone there.'

Alex had pulled on his shoes and was accompanying the youth back to where his father had disappeared. Annie followed more slowly, barefoot, because her sandals would be worse than useless on the rocks.

'I can see him,' Alex told her, 'but he's being buffeted by the waves and hitting against the rocks. He needs to swim out beyond where the waves break and wait for rescue there.'

Alex called to the man, telling him to swim away from the rocks, but he either couldn't hear or had already been injured and the best he could do was stay afloat. Before Annie realised what was happening, Alex was stripping off his clothes, thrusting first his shoes, then his trousers and shirt at Annie, telling her to hold them.

Then he walked out to a high, dry rock and was about to dive when Annie yelled at him.

'Jump, don't dive. It might be shallower than you think.'

So he jumped, while Annie held her breath, first until he surfaced then again until he reached the man and together they swam beyond the curling breakers. She refused to think about the sharks that cruised these shores, or of the way a freak wave could lift the pair and throw them up onto the rocks. Her mind concentrated on willing them both to stay alive.

Then she heard the roar of the jet skis and knew help was on the way, but she still watched tensely as the first jet ski stopped, the driver dropping a flotation device to Alex then lifting the fisherman onto the back of the seat. The driver of the second jet ski helped Alex aboard, and the two machines roared off towards the beach.

Annie followed more slowly, having to pick her way across the rocks, clutching Alex's clothing to her chest. They smelt of him, she realised as she drew warmth and comfort from objects as mundane as a pair of jeans and a shirt. Then she shivered as her body lit again with excitement, imagining enjoying the scent of the man himself just as intimately.

Get real, girl! It's not going to happen. It can't happen.

Can't it?

The mental argument took her to the clubhouse where Alex, wrapped in a blanket, was waiting for her.

'Much quicker to get a ride back,' he teased as she passed over his clothes. And seeing him there, alive and well and teasing, made her remember the clench of terror she'd felt when he'd gone into the water, and she had to bite back an urge to yell at him for being so foolhardy.

'I'm OK,' he said gently, taking her hand and pulling her close enough to drop a kiss on her hair. 'I'm a strong swimmer and could see the safe way to approach the man, or I would never have gone in.'

'OK,' Annie conceded, but he wasn't completely off the hook. 'But don't go doing that kind of hero stuff again! Not when I'm around anyway.'

She thought about it for a moment, then added, 'No, not even when I'm not around. You're far too important to too many people to be putting yourself in danger. And don't bother telling me there was no danger. I was there. I saw it.'

He touched his hand to her shoulder.

'I'll grab a quick shower and get dressed. The lifesavers offered coffee. Do you want a cup?'

Annie shook her head. The words she'd just spoken about Alex putting himself into danger were echoing in her head, together with an insistent little voice suggesting she might be doing it herself—putting Alex into danger by associating with him.

Dennis dangerous?

To her, most probably, but to someone else? She didn't know.

Yet acts in their past and his persistence in trying to find her suggested it was a possibility. It certainly wasn't to finalise divorce proceedings, because she'd started them herself and through a string of different lawyers, all protecting her confidentiality, had had papers served on him.

But all that had done had been to increase the pressure of the private investigators on the family she and her father had left behind.

'Stop frowning. I'm fine!'

Alex's return brought her back to the present.

'Yes,' Annie said, vowing inside herself that she'd have to keep things that way.

This resolution weakened somewhat when he drove his car into the garage behind his house then walked her home down the back lane, no doubt aware of the privacy its dark seclusion offered.

And when he kissed her, which he did at intervals all the way along the lane, Annie's resolve weakened, and she found herself arguing, mentally, that everything would be all right.

CHAPTER SEVEN

ALEX could sense resistance in his companion as they made their way, with frequent stops, towards her house. Not resistance to his kisses—she was too honest and wholehearted in her response! No, it was to do with the past, and whatever it was it haunted Annie as she had haunted him.

They reached her place and he took her to the back door and waited while she unlocked it, calling to Henry to quieten him.

'Would you like a coffee now?' she asked, but lack of sleep and an evening swim had taken their toll and Alex shook his head.

'I'll say goodnight,' he said, and took her in his arms again, kissing her thoroughly, winning sweet, hot kisses in return. But although his body hungered to take things further, his head decreed caution, and he knew it was the right decision at this stage of their relationship.

Especially if Annie was, as he suspected, trying to work out how to tell him it was over before it had begun.

He said goodnight and walked home up the lane, wondering if he was at the two steps forward or one step back part of this relationship. He also found time to wonder why he, with his aversion to emotional dependency, wanted so badly to find out about Annie's past. Wanted so badly to make things right for her.

Wasn't he better off just accepting the Annie of the present, enjoying a relationship with her and letting the past remain where it was—in the past?

Yes was the answer to that question, but he knew that wasn't going to happen. If he had a relationship with Annie then it was already tied to the past.

'Give it up,' he told himself, letting himself in through his back door and bending to lift a delighted Minnie and hush her excited yapping. 'Think about work!'

He dialled the hospital, remembering as the phone rang at the other end that he hadn't told Annie that Amy's new catheter had worked and her kidneys were functioning if not perfectly then well.

The report from the PICU was all good, and

he went off to bed thinking of work, but with a twist of Annie, because he'd be seeing her there in the morning.

'So you see my dilemma, Henry,' Annie said, when she'd filled him in on the Alex situation over a very early breakfast the next morning.

'Just tell the man about Dennis,' her father said, coming in on the tail end of the one-way discussion. 'For Pete's sake, it doesn't reflect badly on you.'

Annie looked at her father. He'd been a policeman for over thirty years, yet he still had no real understanding of how victims of the crimes he'd fought—and now wrote about—felt. This wasn't the first time she'd tried to explain it to him, and it probably wouldn't be the last, but still she tried.

'Dad, you and I were closer than most fathers and daughters are—far closer—but it still took me four years to lift that phone and call you.'

Four years and a stranger's kiss, she amended silently.

'I've known Alex for a week. I *can't* talk to him about it, and even if I could, don't you think he'd run a mile? What sane sensible man would want a woman with so much baggage?'

'A man who loved you, that's who,' her father growled, then he wheeled himself away, not, Annie knew, because he was angry with her but because he, too, still found it hard to cope with what had happened.

Annie said goodbye to her two protectors and walked to work, pleased not to have company because, after a weekend of emotional upheaval, she wanted to get her mind focussed back on the job. Especially as this would be the first week of full-time surgery, the patient first up this morning a young girl Alex had seen last week. Jamie Hutchins was a six-year-old with a previously undiagnosed atrial septal defect, or, in medical shorthand, an ASD, and Alex had scheduled a staff briefing for eight with the operation to start at nine. And because she wanted to be at the briefing, wanted to learn all she could about the work Alex did, here she was heading for work before seven.

And beating Alex, she found when she checked in at the special care unit and learned both patients had enjoyed a peaceful night. But she wasn't the first on duty. As she pushed open the door that led to the suite of open-plan 'offices' she and the doctors used, she saw the light was on, and though her heart skipped an anticipatory beat it was Maggie, not Alex, already at a desk.

'You want a coffee?' Maggie used the question as a greeting. She looked and sounded tired, which puzzled Annie, given the status of their patients.

Annie said yes to coffee and watched Maggie as she poured, seeing tiredness in her actions as well.

'Are you OK?' she asked, and Maggie gave a weary smile.

'When Alex offered me the job up here, I thought it would be a good chance to catch up with my sister, who shifted up here when she married, and get to know her family a bit better. So I asked if I could stay with them until I found somewhere to live.'

'Not a good idea?' Annie sugared her coffee and stirred it.

'A terrible idea,' Maggie told her. 'She's got a spaced-out family—I mean in ages, although Pete, the eldest, is definitely spaced out in other ways. Pete's fifteen and we go down through an eleven-year-old I swear has ADD and twins going through the delightful Terrible Twos.'

'Not much peace and quiet?'

'None!'

'Do you have to stay?'

Maggie shook her head.

'Not really. I think I'm probably as disruptive for them as they are for me. But finding somewhere else isn't all that easy. I don't know the city at all, and have no idea of where to start looking. Somewhere near the hospital, I suppose.'

Annie thought of the house she and her father shared. It had been converted before they'd bought it, so there was a self-contained suite for him downstairs with three bedrooms and two bathrooms upstairs. More than enough room for an extra person.

Yet she felt reluctant to make the offer, and knew the reluctance was tied up with Alex and the relationship they didn't yet have, and might never have, and really, when she thought about it, should never have.

Then she remembered the size of the hearts Alex operated on, and the skill he required from his anaesthetist.

Would an exhausted anaesthetist exhibit the same skill?

How could she *not* offer?

'We've plenty of room at our place and it's just down the road—you can walk to and from work. You don't have to stay for the whole year, but at least it would be handy while you looked around. You can pop down and check the place out during your break between ops and meet my father, and if you like it, I can drive you to your sister's after work and bring you and your gear back home.'

Maggie stared at her.

'You don't know me,' she pointed out, and Annie grinned at her.

'I know you're an excellent anaesthetist and this unit needs one of those, so anything I can do to make your job easier, it's yours.'

Maggie got up from where she'd been slumped behind a desk and came across to give Annie a big hug.

'It needn't be for the whole year,' she assured Annie. 'Just until I get my bearings in Sydney and find somewhere for myself.'

'Whatever suits you,' Annie said, though a sinking feeling in the pit of her stomach told her she'd have a boarder for a year. Where else would Maggie find so ideal a situation?

Maggie was chattering on, so obviously delighted by this change in fortune Annie had to feel happy for her.

'You don't need to drive me. I've got my own car. I'll check out your place at lunchtime then go back to my sister's for tonight to say good-bye to them all, pack my stuff into the car and bring it all over tomorrow.'

'Bring what all over where tomorrow?'

Annie turned at the sound of Alex's voice. Inside, her stomach turned as well, a happy little flip-type somersault.

She smiled at him—a unit co-ordinator greeting the main man smile—and saw a bit more warmth in the smile he gave her back. Although the warmth faded, and the smile grew forced as Maggie happily explained the situation.

'Maggie's coming to live with you?' Alex asked, when Maggie had left the suite to check her new patient.

He sounded hurt, and puzzled, and Annie understood both reactions.

'It might only be temporary,' she said, then remembered why she'd offered.

'Personally, it might not be ideal,' she said, standing up so she could look Alex in the eye, 'but professionally—do you really want a sleep-deprived, twitchy anaesthetist working with you on a child? What else could I do but offer?'

His smile improved, though it was still a wry effort.

'I wish I'd been here. I could have offered to have her at my place. With Phil there already, it wouldn't have mattered and we'd still have had some privacy from work colleagues at your place.'

He brightened considerably.

'We could still do that! I'll offer to have her at my place. She'll be with Jamie. I'll go now.'

He touched Annie on the shoulder and breezed away, obviously delighted with his own brilliance.

But his face was glum again when Annie saw him at the briefing, and he looked far from happy as he explained Jamie's problem, where a hole in the wall between the heart's two upper chambers, the atria, hadn't closed, so blood shunted between the two chambers.

'It causes increased pressure in the right atrium and ventricle, and too much blood flowing into the lungs. Usually the patient suffers few symptoms—a bit of breathlessness and fatigue from time to time. In Jamie's case these didn't become obvious until she started at Little Athletics. Echocardiography has confirmed the hole is there, and her cardiologist has done a cardiac catheterisation as well to determine just where the hole is.'

Alex pointed to his diagram on the whiteboard.

'New technology is being tried for holes in the centre of the atrial wall, and holes are being successfully closed using transcatheter management—inserting wires through a catheter. But Jamie's hole is higher up and the new technique doesn't work, hence the need for an operation.'

'If she's been OK up until now, and is only breathless after running or jumping at Little Athletics, is it worth the risk involved in any operation—particularly open heart where she'll be on a bypass machine for some of it?'

One of the sisters from the special care unit asked the question, and Annie was pleased. For one thing, she'd wondered about it herself, and for another, it meant all the unit staff were becoming increasingly involved in all stages of their patients' operations.

'There's a twenty-five per cent risk of early mortality through pulmonary vascular obstructive disease if it's not repaired and a less than five per cent—in fact, I feel less than one per cent—risk with the operation itself.'

Alex turned back to the board and sketched a small chest.

'We make a much smaller incision than we do for a PDA, only…' He paused, then smiled at them all. 'I have to convert inches to centimetres…say eighty to a hundred centimetres. Then the defect is fixed with either a patch or stitches, depending on what we find. As you said, the child has to go on the heart-lung machine as soon as we open the pericardium, then once the aorta is clamped, we stop the heart beating with cardioplegia, open it up, fix the hole and Jamie's back in business again. Within weeks she should be back at Little Athletics.'

'The results are really good,' Phil added, turning to smile at the sister who'd asked the question. 'You probably won't have her more than a few hours in the PICU, then she'll be moved to the ward.'

'Which reminds me,' Alex said, directing his question to the two nurses present who had been specially selected to work with his patients once they reached the children's post-surgical ward. 'How do you think you'll go, working with our patients exclusively when they're back in the ward with the others?'

'I love the idea of it,' one of them said, while the other nodded agreement. 'It means you can really get to know the children and their families, and there's something special about being chosen as part of the team that's working to make them well again.'

Whatever gloom Alex had shown earlier disappeared, and he beamed at the pair, one male and one female.

'That's great to hear, and don't forget, if you run into administrative trouble at any stage, see Annie and she'll sort it out.'

Annie's turn to smile. Alex could so easily have said to see him, but he had enough faith in her to know she'd handle it.

She just hoped his faith would never prove to be misplaced.

The briefing over, the operating crew headed off for the theatre, the nursing staff back to their places and Annie returned to the office. Alex's prediction that there'd be hospital infighting was already coming true. She had a meeting with the CEO and other surgical co-ordinators at nine-thirty, and guessed pressure would be applied for other surgical services to have equal access to the new theatre.

Not this week they wouldn't, as Alex was booked to operate twice and sometimes three times a day right through until Friday.

'Adult cardiac surgery brings in more dollars than CHD,' the administrator of the adult cardiac programme yelled at her less than an hour later, confirming Annie's prediction.

'But it requires more outlays as well,' Annie shot back, determined to remain calm. 'And takes more hospital resources as patients are hospitalised for longer. Plus, you have to realise that if we operate on infants and children with CHD, it means these children won't need cardiac surgery as adults.'

As soon as the words were out of her mouth, she realised she'd made a mistake. The adult cardiac administrator was a money person through and through, and telling him there'd be fewer patients for him in the future was a challenge to his job security.

'Surely people matter more than dollars!' she stormed at Alex much later when he was foolish enough to ask her how the meeting had gone. 'Surely it's more important to offer children with CHD an opportunity to lead a normal life than to keep up the numbers of adult cardiac patients?'

Alex smiled at her vehemence.

'Of course it is, but you'll find very few administrators within a hospital system—or any system, I suppose—who aren't bent on defending their territory.'

Another smile, and if the first had soothed some of her anger, this second one warmed bits of her left cold from the other man's attitude.

'Weren't you doing just that?' he asked, and the warmth turned to heat.

'No, I wasn't. I was talking people, not numbers or money. I was talking about infants and kids like Jamie who'll go back and run the legs off the others in her age group at Little Athletics. I won't talk numbers and money—I'll keep the figures and use them to prove our worth, but the children and their families will always be my prime concern. And if that's going to make me a bad unit manager then you'd better sack me right now.'

She glared defiantly at him, though she knew a lot of her rage was leftover frustration from the morning's meeting.

'I don't think I could sack you,' he said, another smile, gentle this time, playing around his lips. 'The CEO was most insistent that the job was yours, right from the start. I could ask for just about anything else I wanted, but you were a given. The powers that be in this place have a very high opinion of you.'

'You make it sound as if you didn't want me here!'

He sounded so tired she almost let him off the hook, but if the man this morning had made her angry, this man was making her doubly so, with his assumption that she might not be up to the job. Because she was a woman?

'Were you against me, or against having a woman in the job? Was this a gender issue?'

'Not at all. Actually, I wanted my old administrator, Karen. Annie, are we arguing?'

'Yes,' she told him, then she relented. 'Not arguing precisely, but I'd like to know more about it. It's not exactly confidence-building to think you'd have preferred someone else in this job.'

'Can we talk over dinner?' he suggested hopefully. 'Did you say there was an Italian restaurant near the park? Could we go and argue there? I'm famished, and if I caught the drift of all the arrangements you and Maggie made—I did ask her to stay at my place, by the way, but she refused—this might be my last opportunity for a proper first date.'

'Oh, Alex,' Annie sighed, then, because the longing was still there—strong and hot and insistent—she nodded. 'OK. I'll just phone Dad, because it's closer to walk straight there, then we can cut across the park to come home. It's well lit at night.'

'That's a shame, though there are sure to be shadows. No rocks and fishermen?' Alex said, and Annie smiled at him, knowing he was remembering the interrupted kiss.

'No rocks or fishermen,' she promised.

Definitely two steps forward and one back in this relationship, and right now he was at the back stage, Alex thought as he had a wash before leaving the hospital.

Hell's bells, he hadn't had a date with the woman yet, and he was thinking relationship longevity. And she was as uncertain as a woman could be about *any* relationship—let alone one with him.

And prickly!

Because she'd been hurt before?

He was as certain of that as he was of his own name. If he wasn't careful, he'd blow this before it had even begun, and every instinct told him that would be a very bad thing. A disastrous thing! Muddle-headed he might be, but one thing he was quite clear on—both physically and emotionally he wanted Annie Talbot, and he was pretty sure it wasn't because she was his ghost.

Well, he hoped it wasn't, because he knew from experience that flesh-and-blood women were a lot more bother than ghosts, but in Annie's case he was certain...he smiled to himself...she was worth the effort.

'You don't have to talk about the administrator issue,' Annie said as they left the hospital and she guided him along a path that led around the perimeter of the park. 'It's really none of my business if you wanted to bring her out here.'

Alex was more than happy to accede to this request, but a tightness in Annie's voice suggested he'd better get it settled or he'd be eight steps back.

'Karen Ritchie, my old—no, ex—administrator, is a single mother who has worked sometimes at two or three jobs for the past ten years since her husband left her, to keep her kids and get them through college. They were old enough to be left on their own for a year, with relatives keeping an eye on them, and I thought the year out here, as well as being hard work, would be a treat for Karen.'

'Oh!' Annie said, in a very small voice. 'Yes, she'd have enjoyed it, I'm sure.'

'But, in case you're now feeling bad about Karen, I can see it would have been impossible for her to function efficiently in such a different work environment. I discovered that in Melbourne when I needed administrative help to find my way around the workings of the hospital, and without you in the job here we wouldn't be nearly as far along as we are. So stop worrying about it and let's just go out and eat together and enjoy it.'

Now they were safely over that issue, Alex wondered what they should talk about.

Annie solved that problem.

'I phoned Mayarma, the dog-walker I told you about, and she's more than happy to add Minnie to her mob. She'd like to take her out on her own first to see how she behaves, but I assured her Henry would look after her— Minnie, not Mayarma—if she joins the group.'

'And what do I have to do? How do I arrange things? And what is this wonderful service going to cost me?'

Annie explained the various ways owners left their dogs to be collected, and then named a sum that seemed ridiculously low to Alex.

'That's all she asks?'

Annie nodded.

'It's cash. She's from the Philippines, married to an Australian, and she loves dogs but can't have one as her husband's getting on and could be knocked over by a big dog or trip over a small one. I'll give you her phone number and you can speak to her direct about the arrangements.'

Which sorted out the dogs. Alex wondered if he could turn the subject to more personal matters, but Annie forestalled him with a question.

'Did Maggie tell you why she didn't want to stay with you?'

'No, though I guess it could be something to do with sharing with two men. She might have imagined she'd have to do all the cooking and housework.'

'Mmm.'

Alex waited for an explanation and when none was forthcoming asked, 'That's it? Mmm?'

'It was a considering kind of mmm,' Annie explained. 'An "I'm not sure enough to say anything" kind of mmm.'

'About what?' Alex persisted, realising Annie's conversation, first about the dogs and now about something to do with Maggie, was actually relaxing him quite nicely. It seemed so normal somehow, to be walking like this with Annie and talking trivia.

'About Maggie,' Annie now said, and Alex found he was intrigued. He liked Maggie and greatly appreciated the contribution she made to his work. A good anaesthetist was essential in all operations—but even more critical when working on hearts that could be as small as plums.

But they'd reached the restaurant, and his first whiff of the garlic-scented air turned his thoughts from staff to food.

And once again he made Annie laugh, his indecision over what sauce to have with his *penne* delighting her. Her laughter filled his heart with a heady gladness that went beyond the attraction he felt for her, and filled his mind with a resolve to continue this rather strange courtship.

'It's all very well for you,' he grumbled. 'You probably cook delicious sauces every day of the week. Once I'm past curry, it's steak or steak. Not that you don't have great steak out here in Australia, but it gets a bit boring after a while.'

'You can buy prepared sauces then all you have to do is boil the pasta and heat the sauce and *voilà*, an Italian meal.'

'*Voilà*'s French,' he said, still grumbling, but now because Annie had slipped off the jacket of her suit, revealing a dark green blouse that made her eyes seem greener. And just as he was comparing the colour of the eyes to her blouse the top button popped, revealing a glimpse of a deep shadow between her breasts, so lust replaced the gladness in his heart, while an inner voice—a mean-spirited voice, sharp with jealousy—wondered if she'd had her jacket on or off at the meeting that morning.

'The waitress asked if you'd decided,' Annie said, indicating a young woman who'd materialised by his side.

'I'll have the Matriciana,' he said, and silently congratulated himself on his recovery.

'It's about the only pasta sauce not on the menu. How about you try the Alfredo?'

Annie was just being helpful, but he glowered at her anyway, knowing he couldn't ask what she'd had on at the meeting, suspecting he might be seriously love-struck to be thinking this way, and, as the wine waiter approached, wondering if it would be totally improper behaviour if he reached across the table and did up the wayward button.

He didn't, asking Annie instead if she had a preference in wine, and when she settled on a glass of the house Chianti, he told the waiter he'd have the same. Thankfully, the man departed.

Which left him with Annie, and the revealing neckline of her shirt, which kept drawing his attention as surely as seagulls were drawn to fries at a picnic.

His silence must have stretched a fraction too long.

'You're frowning again. Is it Jamie, or are you still worried about Amy?'

Annie's question—so work-oriented when his mind had been so far away—made him smile.

'If I confess I was thinking of seagulls…' not entirely true but close enough '…would you think I was totally mad?'

'Not totally,' she said, a smile lighting up her face and twinkling in her green-today eyes.

She sat back, obviously waiting for him to explain, but of course he couldn't. Neither could he think of any logical thoughts he might have been having about seagulls.

Apart from them liking fries!

'Jamie came through really well,' he said, reverting to work as an escape from dangerous territory. 'It's hard to tell how older children will react. I think because they understand the concept of an operation, and have some knowledge of what's happening to them, they can be more fearful. I don't know of any studies that have been done to see how that affects recovery, but it would be interesting to test the theory. I had a teenage patient once, and though he was used to having catheters stuck up an artery or vein from his groin, and knew all the process, and watched the screen to see the tube travel to his heart, he told me, years later, how much he'd hated it and how he'd far rather have been knocked out before the procedure took place.'

'Why wasn't it an option?' Annie asked, and Alex smiled to himself. He'd mentioned the case as a diversionary tactic but Annie was so eager to know things he enjoyed these discussions nearly as much as—

Boy! He'd nearly thought 'the popped button' and pulled himself up just in time.

'A lot of older children enjoy being part of their treatment, and we'd assumed that was the case with this youth. However, him telling me how much he hated it was a wake-up call for me, because I'd made an assumption on his behalf. Early on, we did all catheterisations for testing and small ops while the patient was sedated slightly but not out of it, mainly because we didn't have the mild, short-acting anaesthesia we have today. And though we knock the infants out, we'd continued doing the older children with just sedation.'

'Until someone protested?'

Alex nodded. 'Bad medicine, that!' he recalled. 'We should have asked. I always do now, and I make sure the cardiologists—they do most of the caths these days—know how I feel about it. I even gave a paper on it once.'

And as he said the words he remembered where and when he'd given that paper. At the congress at Traders Rest five years ago...

CHAPTER EIGHT

ANNIE knew from the way he looked at her exactly where and when he'd given that paper. And suddenly it was the right time to say something. Not a lot, but enough for Alex to decide if he wanted to keep seeing her or not.

Though it shouldn't be his choice. *She* should decide. And she knew what that decision should be!

But her heart longed for the love she felt might be on offer, while her mind reached out for companionship and her body—well, her body just plain lusted after his!

So she had to say *something*!

She reached out and placed her hand over his, so they both rested on the table. Gave his fingers a squeeze because this could well be the last time she touched him.

Then she withdrew her hand and used it to grip her other one—tightly—in her lap beneath the table so no one could see them twisting anxiously.

She looked at Alex, at the grey eyes that seemed to see right into her soul, and with a heavy heart blurted out the words that needed to be said.

'You've probably guessed I was with someone at the congress. My husband. I left him that night. I haven't seen him since. I started divorce proceedings eighteen months ago, but as I haven't heard from the lawyers I don't know if it's gone through so I could, technically, still be married.'

Alex seemed to be waiting for more, his eyes fixed on her face, then he smiled.

'Are you telling me this in case I have strong feelings about dating married women? Believe me, Annie, if you haven't lived with the guy for five years, I don't think you count as married any more, so you can't escape me that way.'

The teasing tone in his voice warmed all the cold places in her body that thinking about Dennis had produced, but as she replayed all the words—both hers and his—in her head, she realised she was still a long way from explaining exactly where things now stood between her and Dennis.

Not that she knew for certain…

Alex was talking again and she shut away the sudden tremor of fear.

'Annie,' he said gently, 'you must know there are plenty of places in the States where divorce is cheap and easy. Maybe he's divorced you.'

'Maybe,' she said, though she doubted it. When the first of the private investigators had called her father—only two days after she'd left Traders Rest—her father had said Annie was in the US and as far as he knew still with Dennis. Her father had also supplied the man with the name and contact details of the family's solicitors and asked that all contact be made through the firm, which meant there'd always been an address available for the service of papers or for information about a 'quickie' divorce.

'Well, as I said, it doesn't matter,' Alex reiterated. 'Now, would you like to put your hand back on the table? I think on a first date, even in Australia, we'd be allowed to hold hands.'

Annie smiled at the weak joke, but as her fingers were now icy from remembering, she was happy to rest her hand back on the table, appreciating the warmth of his when he placed it on top of hers.

He gave her fingers a squeeze, thanked the waiter who'd brought their wine and then said,

'My mother always said to show interest in one's companions—ask about their jobs and so on. But I know all about your job and you know about mine, and we've already talked about the pets and the food, so I guess we might be up to families. Is it just you and your father in yours? Having had my sister visit last year, I can only see that as a blessing, although I suppose it's been fun having her around. She was an afterthought, my sister. Three boys, then when the youngest was eight along came Frances. I was thirteen, old enough to understand the basic sex education we'd had at school, so you can imagine how horrified I was to realise my mother and father must have done *that* to have produced Frances! Totally grossed me out for a long time!'

Annie laughed.

'I can imagine!' she said, but though her laughter sounded genuine, Alex could still read strain in her face, and the cold fingers nestling beneath his suggested that telling him even the bare bones of her story had upset her.

She lifted her other hand up to pick up her wineglass, tilting it towards him in a toast.

'To the new unit!' she said.

Alex lifted his own glass and clinked it against hers, although he'd always thought the gesture corny.

'Not to the new unit, Annie, but to us!' He raised it higher, then moved it to his lips and took a sip. 'This is a date, remember.'

A slight smile trembled on her lips.

'I'm out of practice at dating,' she said. 'This is the first in a very long time, and I've probably already blown it with a confession about my dubious marital status, and now I'm feeling envious of you, growing up in a family with four kids. You asked if it was just Dad and me in our family, and it is. My mother died when I was eleven, so he and I are closer than most fathers and daughters.'

'Nothing to feel envious about,' Alex assured her, although he felt sorry for anyone who hadn't experienced the kind of upbringing he'd had, and he couldn't imagine not having the close connections he'd retained with his siblings. 'After three boys my mother had always prayed for a girl so she'd have female support within the family, but when Frances came along Mom swore she was more trouble than the three of us put together.'

He could feel Annie's fingers growing warmer and could see the tension draining out of her face. His imagination had provided him with a vivid image of her travelling to the US with her husband, separated from her father— the only close family she had—by an ocean. No mom at home to phone when things were difficult, no supportive letters like the ones he still received from members of his family—though now they were emailed, not posted.

The waitress set their meals on the table. Annie thanked her then took back her hand so she could handle her fork and spoon for some spaghetti-twirling.

'I always order pasta in pieces because I've never mastered that art,' Alex confessed, after admiring her expertise for some time.

'Student meals!' she said. 'I trained in—in a city and Dad was posted in the country at the time, so I shared a flat with three other students. I think we lived on spaghetti for four years. When we were flush we had sauce on it, other times olive oil and garlic.'

She paused then grinned at him.

'Come to think of it, I didn't have many dates back then either!'

Alex knew she was doing her best to keep the conversation light, but her hesitation in mentioning a particular city struck him as off-key and he remembered other times she'd caught herself in conversation.

Were things not finished between herself and her husband in other ways—apart from the divorce? Was she fearful of him finding her?

Mental headshake. OK, so some men did get hung up on ex-wives or ex-partners—you read about it every day in the paper—but Annie had been at the congress with her husband—a congress of cardiologists and cardiac surgeons. Yes, there were ancillary services represented, and a clutch of representatives from drug companies, but to think of any of these people as...

Dangerous?

Annie was talking, about the food and some place at the beach that sold fresh pasta and a variety of sauces.

'It's really delicious, and well worth the drive.'

'We could go together on Saturday—if all's well at work,' Alex suggested, then knew from the arrested look in Annie's eyes that she'd mentioned the place as offhand conversation.

And he knew, in her mind, this wasn't just a first date. It was a final one as well.

But why? He tried to get inside her head. To work out what might have happened to make her so determined not to get involved with him when it was equally obvious she liked him.

And, from her response to his kisses, felt an attraction towards him.

She'd had a bad experience with marriage— that was obvious—but that wasn't at all rare these days. People he knew had been married three or four times and had very few hang-ups about it. He didn't think that kind of short-term arrangement would suit him, but still…

He considered how things must have been. Marrying fairly young then travelling to the US where her husband had been her sole support— probably, if she hadn't worked, her sole contact with the outside world. If things had been difficult between them, she'd have been truly isolated. Living in the most civilised country in the world, yet so alone she may as well have been on the moon.

The waiter appeared to ask if he'd like more wine, and he realised he'd been sipping at his glass, emptying it, as he thought. He thanked the man and was about to wave him away when he realised Annie's glass was also empty.

'Would *you* like another glass of wine? Don't stop because I did. I'm always aware I could be called in, so I usually stop at one—on rare occasions two.'

She shook her head and the waiter went away, then she smiled the slightly mischievous smile that made her eyes sparkle.

'Just because I didn't have a mother, it doesn't mean I wasn't warned about drinking too much on a first date. I think my father, having been on the other side of the dating game, probably knew more about it than any woman ever would. He typed up lists of warnings he not only read out to me before I went out the door but also taped all over the place.'

Alex chuckled at the image of fatherly concern.

'How did it start? Boys are only after one thing?'

Annie relaxed for the first time since they'd sat down and Alex had mentioned the paper he'd given at the congress.

'That was the first, fourth, sixth, eighth and eleventh, if I remember rightly. It was something he repeated with such regularity it confused me more than it helped. To begin with, I thought the ''one thing'' was a kiss, so for my first three years at high school, on the rare dates friends arranged for me, I refused to let any of the boys kiss me. Then the story went around that I had some terrible lip disease—far worse than herpes—and I didn't have to worry about saying no because no one ever asked me.'

Alex laughed, and Annie felt absurdly pleased that she could make him laugh.

'Did your father spread the rumour?' he asked, and Annie joined in his laughter.

'I often wondered,' she admitted, and with the tension eased between them they finished their meals, refused coffee and set out to walk home through the park.

'Terrible lip disease all cleared up now?' Alex asked, slowing their pace as they drew near a patch of shadow beneath a spreading, leafy tree.

'I think so,' Annie said, allowing him to turn her in his arms, wanting his kiss so badly she refused to think past the here and now. 'And if it isn't,' she added softly, moving closer so he'd know she wanted to be kissed, 'you've already been contaminated.'

He bent his head until only a breath of air separated them.

'Not contaminated, Annie,' he whispered into that tiny space. 'Addicted.'

Annie's lips responded first, remembering delight imprinted on them from the previous kisses, then her body warmed and heat glowed within it, and the longing grew so strong she knew there was no way she could resist a second date and then a third and whatever all of this was leading to.

And though doubt and guilt still existed in her head, what was happening in other parts of her enabled her to ignore them, offering up feeble excuses about Alex only being here for a year, and wasn't it time she got some pleasure out of life, and why shouldn't she enjoy his company for a while?

'Ah,' Alex said, a long time later, lifting his head and taking a deep breath. 'I thought I'd lost you there for a while, but once you put your mind to a kiss, Annie Talbot, I can only say you do a first-rate job.'

He smoothed her hair back from her face, cupped his hand around her jaw and cheek and looked into her eyes, though she knew it was too dark for him to see more than a blurred outline of her face.

'I've stopped kissing you and I'm making this ridiculous light conversation, because if that kiss had gone on for much longer, I'd have had to ravish you right here beneath this tree. And while I don't know about Australian customs, public exhibitions of lovemaking are not looked on kindly by the police in most places where I've lived.'

'No,' she said, though not sure if it should have been a yes. Not that Alex seemed to care because he took it as an invitation to kiss her again, this time on the forehead, and temple, and on her eyelids now she'd closed them to enjoy the sensation of his lips against her skin.

'So, where do we go from here? And I'm not talking about tonight, I'm talking about our dating, which, as I pointed out to you this morning, is going to get more complicated once Maggie moves in.'

His statement reminded Annie of his reaction to the news that morning, although what difference having Maggie in the house would make she wasn't sure.

Unless, as Annie had once suspected, Maggie was interested in Alex. And why wouldn't she be? He was good-looking, a top surgeon and, as far as Annie could make out, very nice. No signs of ruthlessness so far!

He was also a man, and he'd been in Melbourne for six months and busy at the hospital so most of the women he'd met would have been at or through work. Had he dated Maggie?

If he had, it could certainly get awkward!

'Why will it get more complicated?' Annie asked, thinking a direct question was the most tactful way of sorting things out.

Because she was still wrapped in his arms she felt rather than saw Alex's shrug.

'I don't know exactly, except that relationships between colleagues can sometimes turn sour, then that leads to disharmony in the team.'

'But if it's things turning sour that worries you, then you and I shouldn't be seeing each other at all, and Maggie living at my place makes no difference whatsoever.'

'No, I put that badly.' Alex pulled her closer. 'I've worked with too many husband-and-wife teams that work perfectly to ever denigrate them. And, anyway, it was just an excuse—a stupid, thoughtless excuse. My bad reaction to the news was a man thing—the thing your father wrote so often on your list. It's not all I want from you, Annie, you must know that, but, yes, one day I would hope our relationship progresses to a sexual one and, being a man, I think in practical terms of where that will take place.'

'And you've got Phil at your place, so my place was the obvious answer, but now I'll have Maggie at my place and it will be awkward.'

Annie put his thoughts together in the only way that seemed logical, but there were still holes large enough to drive a bus through.

'But I have Dad at my place anyway,' she began, then light dawned and she drew away from him.

'You don't mind Dad knowing you're staying over at my place, but you don't want other members of the team to know we're seeing each other? Or is it that you don't want them knowing we're having sex?'

Alex tried to draw her close again, but when she stiffened he immediately released her.

'Annie, it isn't that. Well, I guess it is, but I was thinking of you as well as myself. I was wondering how you'd feel about me emerging from your bedroom and running into Maggie in the bathroom.'

'I have my own bathroom,' Annie snapped, angry with him but also understanding the problem and angry with herself for causing it.

But she couldn't have not offered Maggie a place to stay!

'Well, in the hall, or anywhere, just as it could be awkward for you running into Phil at my place. It's an embarrassment factor, nothing else.'

He put his hands on her shoulders and applied just enough pressure to let her know he wanted to hold her. And this time she let him draw her close again.

'I do understand,' she muttered. 'I'm just cranky that it's all so muddled.'

She snuggled against his body.

'Anyway, it might never happen. I like you, Alex—a lot—but for all kinds of reasons, including the bathroom scenario, this should be a first and last date. I'm really not a datable person. Too much baggage, too many secrets, and if there's one thing I've carried with me from my father's lists of behaviour, it's the one about not having secrets in a relationship. I'm not talking little secrets, like being scared of snakes, but big secrets.'

She sighed, so happy in his arms, so sorry it couldn't be for ever—or even for a year—but knowing it couldn't.

Shouldn't!

'Apart from snakes, I doubt there's much you're scared of, Annie Talbot,' he murmured, pressing kisses against her hair and her ear, teasing at the lobe, making Annie's body squirm with delight.

But hearing the name that wasn't her name—hearing the gentle way he spoke the words 'Annie Talbot'—reminded her that what she'd said was right, and this relationship shouldn't—couldn't—be.

Until he kissed her lips again, seducing not only her body but her common sense as well.

It took a long time to walk home, and even longer to say goodnight in the shadows of the camellia bush.

'I really must go,' Alex said at last. 'I want to slip up to the hospital. I know they'd page me if they needed me, but in a new situation, with staff that don't know me and might worry about disturbing me, I like to check things for myself.'

'Like whether the tubes and wires are all in the right place,' Annie teased, knowing how insistent Alex was about the particulars of patient care.

'Exactly,' he said, lifting her hair and finding a new place to kiss, just beneath her ear, where the nerves must be connected directly to her nipples as they peaked in an exquisite agony of delight.

'Go,' she said, 'or we'll be embarrassing ourselves on my front porch.'

'I could come back,' he suggested, his voice hoarse with need, but without much expectation.

'Best not,' Annie said. 'My father's list didn't exactly say "don't put out on a first date" but I'm sure it was implied somewhere there.'

She spoke lightly, hoping Alex would accept it as a joke, but in her heart of hearts she knew that if she took this relationship with him any further she'd be lost—so under his spell, or the spell of the attraction between them, she'd never be able to push him away.

Alex grunted and kissed her once more on the lips, then touched his hand to her cheek again and said goodnight.

Annie leaned against the porch railing and watched until he disappeared into the shadows at the end of the road.

Her body ached with frustration while her mind churned with doubts and questions to which she had no answers.

Eventually, she unlocked the door and went inside. Seeing the light on in the kitchen, she found her father reading at the big table, Henry asleep across his feet.

'Do you think Dennis is dangerous?' she asked, the biggest question in the churn popping straight out.

Her father looked at her for a long moment, then he shook his head.

'You worried about what you might be getting that fellow into?'

Annie nodded.

'I think you've got reason to be,' her father said, then he sighed. 'Though I don't know for sure, Annie. We've never known for certain why Dennis has been so keen to find you, but my experience and that of other people on the force, and people I've spoken to in Social Services who deal with this stuff—it all points to someone as persistent in trying to find you as Dennis has been, being at least borderline dangerous. What he's done, with his private investigators roaming around the country, is tantamount to stalking. Stalking by proxy but still stalking. You took nothing from him—no money, clothes, passport, nothing—so it's not as if he's looking for you to get something back.'

'Is he still looking do you think? Has Uncle Joe said anything?'

Her father looked surprised.

'Why mention Uncle Joe?'

Annie smiled—a sad effort but a smile nonetheless.

'Dad, did you think I wouldn't figure out why you go off on your solo jaunts once or twice a month? Why you drive up to the Gold Coast or fly down to Melbourne? Why would you do it, if not to contact Uncle Joe from somewhere out of Sydney to find out how everyone is?'

'Think you're clever, I suppose,' her father growled. 'I assumed you'd think I'd headed off for a naughty weekend. But you're right, I do keep in touch with Joe. I let him know we're OK and find out what's happening over in the west. I phone him at work—no way all the calls to the internal investigations division in Perth could be traced—but I phone from other cities just in case.'

He sighed.

'Dennis is still looking. One of those PIs visited your grandmother just last week. A different firm this time. Your gran asked him to leave his card and whether his firm had contacts in the US because she hadn't heard from you for a long time and she thought she might hire someone to find you.'

'Good old Gran. I'm glad she knows we're OK,' Annie said, thinking of the tears she'd shed over not being able to contact her grandmother.

But right from the start, when a private investigator rather than Dennis himself had contacted her father, two days after she'd left the hotel, he'd been insistent she shouldn't see or talk to anyone from her past. She'd been cared for by the wife of the policeman she'd first spoken to and then passed on to an organisation that miraculously looked after women in her situation.

Through them and, she was pretty sure, illegally, she'd eventually flown back to Australia, or rather Annie Talbot had flown back. Then a similar though much smaller organisation in Australia had helped her father disappear—though as a policeman he'd needed less help—to re-emerge in Sydney as Rod Talbot, and take up the writing he'd played at for years, scoring a hit with his first published novel.

'But we're off the subject. Am I putting Alex in danger by seeing him?'

She sat down on the floor by her father's chair and rested her head on his knee.

'I like him so much,' she confessed quietly, 'that I couldn't bear for harm to come to him through me.'

Her father stroked her hair and Henry, perhaps sensing her deep need, moved so he could put his big head on her lap.

'I can understand that, love,' her father said. 'But maybe it's not your decision to make. Maybe you have to tell him all about it, and let him decide for himself.'

Annie thought about that for a while then shook her head.

'That's not going to work, Dad, because if we're not absolutely certain there's a risk to us, why would he think there'd be one to him? We don't *know* Dennis means us harm, and most men, I would think, confronted with my pathetic tale, would go all macho and protective, when in reality they should run for their lives.'

'Perhaps literally,' her father said, his voice sober with the gravity of the situation as he knew it.

Annie sat for a while longer, enjoying the closeness with her father but reliving the regrets she still felt that he'd given up so much for her.

'I'm happy, love,' he said, reading her thoughts in the deep sigh she gave. 'Happier than I would have been if I was still in the force—not that they'd have wanted to keep a broken-down old crock like me. I've discovered writing, and I love it. I lead a full life—you know that. My jaunts away aren't purely to phone your uncle!'

Annie chuckled, comforted by the words, but her laughter died when she reminded herself she was no closer to finding a solution to the Alex dilemma than she had been when she'd kissed him goodnight.

CHAPTER NINE

LOOKING back, Alex wondered if he'd angered the gods in some way the night he'd eaten at the Italian restaurant with Annie. The week turned into a nightmare, beginning with little Amy's condition deteriorating to the extent where he had to admit her abused little heart just hadn't been able to cope with the most recent operation.

First thing Tuesday morning he met with her parents, and together they decided to put her on the list for a donor heart.

'Will you arrange it?' he said to Annie later. 'It will have to be a very small heart—she's such a tiny thing.'

'I can arrange the listing but, because patients from Jimmie's who required transplants were sent across to the Children's, I've never had much to do with the donor programme. How often would very small donor hearts become available?'

She'd zeroed on the heart of his despair.

'Not once while I was in Melbourne. I don't know the Australian figures but, I imagine, given the small population, donor programmes are struggling for organs. For that matter, so are the programmes in the US. The wait can be months or even years.'

'And Amy won't last years and possibly not even months,' Annie said softly. 'Look, leave it with me. I'll find out about priorities and what kind of waiting list there is and get back to you later today.'

Alex touched her shoulder by way of thanks—how could he not touch her when they were so close?—but his mind remained on work as they went through his schedule for the week.

'I'll see you later,' he said, leaving the office to meet the staff before the first op of the day. But in fact, though he did see her during that day and the next three, there was little time for social talk and no time at all for even thinking about dating.

'I'm whacked,' Maggie said to Annie, coming into the office early on Friday evening and finding Annie still at her desk. 'I was going to offer to cook dinner for you and Rod tonight as between you you've been feeding me all week, but

I haven't the strength to pick up a stirring spoon, let alone a knife to slice anything, so how about I take the two of you out? Rod was telling me about a Thai restaurant nearby.'

Annie hesitated for a moment, then, realising she couldn't say, *I was rather hoping Alex might ask me out*, and as Alex himself had been conspicuous by his absence, she nodded.

'Sounds like a plan,' she said, ignoring the crunch of disappointment inside her chest and telling herself it was for the best.

Maggie left to check the special care unit where her patients from the three ops they'd done that day were under the care of the intensivist, and Annie stared at the wall for a while, wondering just where Alex was. They'd barely seen each other all week. No, that wasn't true— she saw him a dozen times a day, but it was always rushed and there were work-related issues to be discussed and reviewed.

'Wondering where to eat tonight?' Phil's voice made her turn. 'Come out with me. Rumour has it there's a first-class Thai restaurant nearby and, as the local, it's your duty to lead me to it.'

Annie grinned at him, pleased as ever to see Phil, who could lighten up the dreariest day with a joke and a wink of his blue eyes.

'I'm leading Maggie to it tonight,' she told Phil. 'And my dad. Why don't you join us?'

She'd have liked to have included Alex in the invitation but didn't want to hear Phil tell her Alex had other plans—which he must have if Phil was at a loose end.

Though Phil at a loose end seemed strange as well.

'Join you and Maggie and your father? That's hardly a date!'

'No, that's why I suggested it,' Annie told him. 'Come on, it'll be fun, and we'll eat early so you can go gallivanting off later if you want to.'

'Can't,' Phil said gloomily. 'The boss has me on duty all weekend. I don't know for sure, but I suspect he has "plans".'

Phil used his fingers to give the word inverted commas, and the clench Annie had felt in her heart earlier became a gut-wrench.

'Good for him,' she managed, though she didn't mean a word of it. Betrayal, that's what it was! So what if she'd said Monday night might have been a first and last date—he didn't have to take it literally.

'You're looking at the wall again,' Phil said, and she turned and forced a smile to her lips.

'Helps me think,' she said, 'and right now I need to think because I've got to check a few things out before I leave the office and if I don't get on with it, we'll never eat.'

She looked at her watch. It was already close to seven.

'Shall we say eight o'clock at my place? We can walk from there. I'll phone and make a booking for eight-thirty.'

Maggie returned and waited while Annie finished what she was doing, then they walked home together.

'No word on a heart for Amy?' Maggie asked as they left the hospital.

'No, but she's only been listed for a few days. I speak to the donor programme manager at the Children's every day. I'm working on the squeaky wheel principle, but Amy's not top of the list. There's a little boy who's been waiting over a month for a heart and lungs.'

'But that's come up,' Maggie told her. 'This afternoon. Alex got a call while we were in Theatre, and when he called back it was a surgeon asking Alex if he'd assist. A team was flying out to some place in western New South Wales to harvest the organs and bring them back, and Alex is already over at the Children's, going through the op with the other surgeons. If Amy's next on the list, that's good, isn't it?'

It was, but Annie was too busy considering the other information. No wonder Alex hadn't asked her out to dinner! How pathetic was she to be getting uptight about it?

'But if the phone call came while Alex was operating, why doesn't Phil know about it? He was complaining that Alex had him on call all weekend, and hinting Alex had a big social weekend planned.'

They were nearly home now. In fact, they were passing Alex's house, and Maggie turned to look at it.

'Phil wasn't in Theatre for the last op. Alex had one of the residents there for experience.' Her voice was distracted and once again Annie wondered if Maggie harboured tender feelings towards their boss. 'And I think Alex did have plans for the weekend, but now he'll probably spend the two days over at Children's. He's always on edge when his patients are post-op and he feels better when he's close to them.'

He has post-op patients here, too, Annie wanted to say, but she knew today's list had all been minor repairs and replacements and all their patients, with the exception of Amy, were stable. She was just feeling peevish because she'd seen so little of him that week. Now a whole weekend stretched ahead of her, with no gleam of hope that they might somehow get together.

Maggie was talking about her experiences working with Alex in Melbourne, and how much she'd learned through being part of his team.

'I'd love to work in the US or in England, and this experience has been so advantageous for me.'

'Is work all you want out of life?' Annie asked, because Maggie sounded so sure and enthusiastic and because, although she herself had thought a career was all she wanted, lately she'd been aware it wasn't enough. Not nearly enough.

Although as things stood, it was all she could have…

'No, of course not. I want marriage, and children, but that won't stop me working. I think I'd make a terrible stay-at-home mother, and you can get such good nannies these days, I really don't see the point of giving up a career I love. That's the good thing about anaesthetics. I can keep working almost up until I have the baby, then take say two months' maternity leave to feed the little scrap when it arrives, then back to work. Actually, if I can time the feeds right, and the hospital has child-care facilities, I can keep right on breastfeeding for months.'

Annie considered this juggling of priorities and while she was aware it could work—and probably would for the efficient and determined Maggie—she wasn't sure it was the way she'd go if she decided to have a family.

She shook her head as she followed Maggie up the path to her house. For five years marriage and a family had been the furthest thing from her mind. Her career had been the be-all and end-all of her existence. Now, suddenly, she was going mushy over getting married and having babies—something she knew wasn't possible. The getting-married part anyway—she wasn't sure if having babies was or wasn't possible—but it certainly wasn't an option.

Henry, having greeted Maggie, now came gambolling towards her.

'Not an option for you either, is it boy?' she said, rubbing her hand over his head and scratching behind his ears.

Inside, she could hear her father laughing with Maggie, and knew she should be happy with the way things were going. The job was great, the unit was working successfully, although with so many of their post-op patients now on the ward she wanted to go up there later and see how the night staff were handling things.

Everything should be rosy—and would have been if a stupid emotion called love hadn't come along and tapped her on the shoulder, reminding her she was a flesh-and-blood woman as well as an efficient administrator.

Maybe Alex was right, and he should have brought his own administrator, then all this would never have happened.

Phil arrived while she was upstairs, showering and changing, and she came downstairs to find him sitting with Maggie and her father, discussing ways to kill off unwanted relations.

'Not me, I hope,' she said to her father, who grinned at her.

'No, Phil's dotty grandfather who has gone to live with his mother and is, in Phil's opinion, sending his mother to an early grave.'

'They're after me for info on undetectable drugs,' Maggie offered, 'but I'm keeping my secrets in case I ever need to knock off a surgical fellow or two.'

She smiled at Rod, not at Phil, as she said it, but something in her tone made Annie wonder if perhaps Phil, not Alex, was the object of Maggie's affections. The idea gave her something to ponder as they walked down the road towards the restaurant, Maggie walking beside Rod's electric wheelchair, Phil beside Annie.

I'll make sure it's the other way around as we come home, Annie decided, pleased to have someone else's relationship to think about, but as they ate their way through a sumptuous feast, she began to wonder if she'd got it right. Maggie seemed to be flirting more with Rod than Phil, while Phil was close to embarrassing Annie with his attentions.

'So, shall we go on to a night spot? I'm on call so I'm not drinking, but there's no embargo on dancing,' Phil said, when Maggie had insisting on settling the bill and they were about to leave. He turned to Rod. 'Can that machine dance? Having seen wheelchair athletes playing basketball, I never assume there's anything a person can't do.'

'Damn, I didn't bring my dancing chair tonight,' Rod told him. 'But that's OK. I've a deadline to meet and should have been working anyway. You young folk go ahead.'

Maggie seemed eager, which suited Annie just fine.

'You two go. There are a couple of good nightclubs over at Bondi, which is closer than going into the city. But count me out. I want to go up to the hospital to see how the night shift are handling the kids we have on the ward. It's the first time they'll have had a full caseload.'

Phil protested, but by now Maggie had offered to drive so he could hardly pull out. They all walked home together, then Maggie led Phil through to the back yard where she kept her car in a paved area next to the garage. Annie watched them go, wondering why Phil had been at a loose end that evening—and whether his preference for blondes would stop him seeing what a nice person Maggie was.

Saturday was well and truly started by the time Alex, exhausted after a six-hour operation that had taken place after an already busy day, drove carefully home. Not wanting to leave until he knew the little boy they'd operated on was OK, he'd slept for a couple of hours in an on-duty room at the Children's but, as ever, the short sleep had made him feel worse than no sleep at all.

Minnie greeted him with hysterical delight and, knowing he wouldn't sleep again immediately and needing some exercise and fresh air, he clipped on her lead and led her outside, heading for the park. He paused only momentarily outside Annie's gate, though why she'd be up at six in the morning on a Saturday, he didn't know.

Minnie dragged him on, stopping to sniff at every second fence post but never deviating far from the path to the park.

Alex smiled at her antics—and at his thoughts. One of the adult cardiac surgeons had told him about a hideaway not far from Sydney in an area called the Blue Mountains, where one could rent luxury cabins for a weekend. Gourmet meals were delivered, the cabins had full facilities, including a glass-walled spa that looked out over great views, and in his mind he'd begun planning to take Annie there this weekend.

It was rushing things, he knew, but he'd sensed she was drawing away from him and he felt a need to rush. A weekend away would get them from first date to fifth or sixth and they'd both have the opportunity to relax far from the pressures of work.

He'd even booked—tempting fate, he knew—because Annie could so easily have said no when he sprang it on her late Friday afternoon.

But instead of springing anything on Annie, he'd been asked to assist at Children's and known he couldn't say no.

They'd reached the park and he bent to let Minnie off her lead, wondering, as he did it, if this was wise. Without Henry to bring her back, would she come?

Excited yipping from his dog and a gruff, deep bark from behind some bushes solved his problem. Henry was here! Was Annie with him or did Rod sometimes walk the dog?

He followed the path and his questions were answered. Annie was sitting on the seat they'd sat on last week, her head tipped back so the early morning rays of the sun gave her skin the subtle sheen of gold.

Alex stood and looked at her for a moment. He was too far away to see the freckles on her nose, but his imagination painted them in for him. And suddenly, tired as he was, he wanted to kiss those freckles—to kiss Annie—here in the park, in the sunshine.

Had his thoughts arrowed across the space between them and disturbed her? He hoped not, because she might not welcome kisses in the park at the break of day. But, for whatever cause, she straightened and turned to look around, seeing him coming towards her and smiling a greeting.

Maybe she wouldn't mind kisses in the park at daybreak!

'Alex! How are you? How's your patient with the new heart and lungs? Did everything go all right?'

She stood up to meet him and put out her hand, so it seemed only natural to use it to pull her towards him so he could try the kiss option.

No sign of her minding, although Henry's bark suggested he thought it bad form to be behaving in this manner in his park.

Annie pulled away from him, but he kept his arm around her as they sat down on the seat.

'And how did you know about the heart-lung saga?' He was studying her as he asked the question and saw lines of weariness in her face, as if she, too, had had little sleep.

'Phil,' she said succinctly, then explained they'd all had dinner together.

Alex felt a tightening in his gut, but refused to accept he might be jealous of Phil having dinner with Annie, even as part of a group.

'It went well?'

Annie's repetition of the question reminded him he hadn't answered, so he told her all about the operation and that they were tentatively hopeful it would have a great result.

'Great result? That's wonderful! Far better than a good result?'

Tired as he was, Alex had to smile at her enthusiasm.

'It is,' he said, still smiling, because sitting in the sun with Annie was just about as good as life could get. Right now, that was. Later, he was sure, it could get a whole lot better. He even began to wonder if the cabin in the mountains might still be available.

'So I think they might be having second thoughts.'

'Who might be having second thoughts about what?' he demanded, as the scrap of conversation he had heard brought him back from thoughts of sharing a spa bath with Annie while enjoying views over the mountains.

'The Carters,' Annie explained, then she turned to look at him. 'Have you had any sleep? Did I wake you up just then? I was telling you I went up to the hospital after dinner, just to see how the staff were coping with our patients on the ward, and ended up spending the night with Amy's mother. She's distressed about Amy's condition—not about her not getting better but whether keeping her alive in the hope we'll get a heart for her is the right thing to do.'

Annie paused, because she understood the deeper implications behind Mrs Carter's doubts but wasn't sure how to explain them to Alex.

'It happens,' he said tiredly. 'We tell parents all we can, we see they get whatever help and counselling they need, but it's still up to them. And honestly, Annie, it tears at my heart to see a child like Amy deteriorating daily. I don't know what's the right thing to do—I don't even know what I'd decide for my own child, because I don't have a child. So when a parent asks me what I'd do, I'm only guessing.'

He drew her closer, and she relished the feel of his body against hers and stayed close while she tried to tell him more.

'What's really upsetting Mrs Carter is the thought that another child has to die for Amy to get a heart. She's having strong ethical doubts about the rightness of it.'

Annie sighed and snuggled closer, although the last thing she should be doing was snuggling close to Alex.

'What makes it worse is I can understand where she's coming from, Alex, so I wasn't the right person to be helping her. It's not a religious doubt, but something that sits a little uneasily with me. Not transplants in general—I'm a registered organ donor and should I suddenly drop dead, I'd be happy for surgeons to use whatever bits of me they can—but to be waiting for a baby to die somewhere—to think about the parents of that baby—yes, I can see why Amy's mother is having doubts.'

Alex stroked her hair, a gentle, soothing caress that eased her tension and her tiredness.

'We all think of that—think of the other baby,' he said slowly, 'and each of us, in our own way, has to come to terms with it. Like so many things in life, Annie, there's no absolute right or wrong. No rules to guide us in decision-making. Oh, there are ethical considerations and laws that govern the use of human organs, but it comes down to personal decisions every time.'

'Personal decisions,' Annie echoed. 'That makes it sound so easy, but aren't personal decisions often the hardest ones to make?'

Alex sensed they were no longer talking about Amy Carter, or even transplants, and once again he cursed the fate that had ordained he'd needed to operate last night.

He was about to suggest they go to the mountains anyway—now, today—but reality intruded and in a not-so-difficult personal decision he knew he'd be useless if he didn't get some sleep. And before he could do that he would have to go up to the hospital and see the Carters once again.

Annie must have guessed their tryst was over for she whistled Henry, who brought Minnie with him as he came.

'If I don't go home right now, I'll fall asleep on this seat and be arrested for vagrancy,' she said, turning towards him and resting her palm against his cheek. 'And you need sleep as well. Not that you'll go weakly home and fall into bed. You'll go and see the Carters, won't you? I shouldn't have told you until later. Or I could have told Phil—let him talk to them.'

He turned his head so he could kiss her palm.

'Phil's good but it's me who should be there for them,' he told her.

Annie nodded, and he realised she understood exactly how he felt. Would always understand…

He walked her home, suggested maybe they could get together later in the day and read her refusal in her face before she shook her head.

'I promised Maggie I'd take her into town to show her where the best shops are. She suggested we stay there and catch a show.'

Annie didn't sound all that certain about these arrangements, but Alex didn't press the point. The way things were going, he probably wouldn't get to bed until the afternoon and might then, with any luck, sleep right through. But he wasn't going to give up on the entire weekend.

'Tomorrow?' he asked hopefully, and Annie smiled.

'Maybe tomorrow,' she said. 'One thing I'm learning with this unit—and that's to count on the unexpected.'

Alex had to accept that, then, aware the day was getting older and people were around, he dropped a quick kiss on her lips and took himself and Minnie home.

'All right for you,' he grumbled at the little dog when she had a drink of water then collapsed on her bed in the kitchen. 'I've got to go to work before I can have a sleep.'

He went upstairs to freshen up with a shower, passing Phil's closed door on his way to his bedroom.

'All right for Phil, too,' he muttered to himself. 'Dining out with my girl then sleeping in next morning.'

But the 'my girl' thought lifted his spirits somewhat, and before he had a shower he sat down at the computer and shot off an email to his former administrator, still working at the hospital where he'd worked previously. If anyone could dig out some details on the current life and whereabouts of Dennis Drake, Karen could. Do it discreetly, he warned her, not wanting to stir up any trouble for Annie with his enquiries.

CHAPTER TEN

ANNIE went home, had breakfast with Henry and her father, then took herself off to bed. Maggie's door was shut but a note on her bed told her she had cried off the shopping expedition, the only explanation being, 'Late night, need sleep.'

Which meant Annie *could* have got together with Alex after all!

But while her mind grumbled over this change of plans, her body told her it was a good idea. She needed sleep more than she needed a shopping trip or a 'maybe' date with Alex.

She woke to evening darkness—she'd slept all day?—and the smell of something delicious cooking downstairs, and lay for a few minutes, savouring the exotic and unfamiliar aromas. Spices certainly, and a sweet smell—honey?

Tantalised tastebuds drove her out of bed and into the shower. She pulled on sweatpants and an old T-shirt and headed downstairs to find out what was cooking—literally.

The noise level from the kitchen suggested more than one person was involved in producing the tempting meal, but if for one moment she'd imagined Alex was one of those present, she'd have shot back upstairs and changed. Dating or not, a girl had some pride!

But Alex's voice didn't reach her above the hubbub and she wandered in to find him and Phil sitting at the table with her father, Alex with his single glass of red wine in front of him, Phil and her father each with a light beer, while a flushed, and very pretty-looking, Maggie wove some magic spell around the stove.

'This kitchen has never smelled so good,' she said, trying to still the heart flutters finding Alex there had caused.

'Ours never looks so good,' Phil added, looking from her to Maggie. Was he flirting with both of them?

'What smells so delicious?' Annie asked, moving closer to where Maggie was stirring something in an earthenware pot that certainly wasn't out of Annie's kitchen.

'It's a *tagine*—a Moroccan dish. Actually the name of the pot is a *tagine* and that's where the dish gets its name. It's made with lamb and apricots and prunes and spices, and I serve it with couscous.'

'It smells delicious and I can see it's drawn some of the neighbours in. I just can't imagine why the whole street isn't here to enjoy it.'

'I was invited,' Phil said. 'Saw your father earlier and he asked me over. Alex just came along.'

Annie was aware Alex was watching her, but the whole situation had got beyond her. She opened the fridge door, found a bottle of white wine and waved it in the air, asking Maggie to join her in a glass.

'Not me,' Maggie said. 'I had my weekly quota of wine last night.'

Her voice sounded tense, but as Annie knew *she'd* be more than tense if she was trying to cook something complicated in front of an audience—particularly this audience—she thought nothing of it.

The meal was as delicious as it had smelt, the subtle blend of flavours perfectly complemented by the bland grain. But for Annie it was spoilt by the company—or, more truthfully, by the behaviour of the company.

Because, with the exception of her father, they were all colleagues, she asked Alex about his talk with the Carters, but he dodged the question, talking instead to Maggie about the recipe for the *tagine*.

Phil, also, had no intention of turning this into a work night, flirting with Annie right through the meal and making her feel uncomfortable and embarrassed. Making her also the target of strange looks from both Maggie and Alex.

Surely Alex must know Phil well enough to realise he was joking—that it was just Phil being Phil.

The looks from Maggie were even more puzzling for, as the evening went on, Maggie grew quieter and quieter in spite of the praise heaped on her for her meal. In the end she stood up.

'I cooked so someone else washes up,' she announced, and she walked out of the room.

Phil and Alex both turned to watch her go, while Annie tried to work out when the mood around the table had changed from light-hearted fun to uneasy silences and sideways glances.

'Us men will stack the dishwasher. Alex and Phil can clear away and rinse and pass things to me—I'm at a better level for stacking.' Rod made the suggestion and with a slight movement of his head suggested Annie should, unobtrusively, leave the room and follow Maggie. Find out what was wrong!

Annie waited for a few minutes then as Alex stood up to clear the table, she headed upstairs. She tapped on Maggie's door, and when Maggie didn't answer Annie opened it, just a crack, and asked if she could come in.

A huge sigh from inside, where Maggie was face down on the bed.

'What's up? That was a fantastic meal, so it can't be that. What's happened?'

Maggie sat up, sighed again and rubbed her hands across her cheeks. She hadn't, as far as Annie could tell, been crying, but her expression—her whole attitude—told of despair.

'Phil's happened—that's what!' Maggie said bitterly. 'Oh, Annie, why are we women such fools? Damn it, I'm thirty-two, old enough to know better, but, no, I've been attracted to Phil from the first day we met, and as far as he's concerned I could be wallpaper.'

She sat up straighter and ran her fingers through her hair.

'The bloody man flirts with every female he comes across and has done since I first met him, but me—no! Wallpaper, you see.'

She sighed again before continuing.

'So what happens last night? We end up clubbing together. I *knew* he'd asked you out last
night—that's how come he was in the party in
the first place—but, no, we go off together and,
because he's Phil, of course he puts the hard
word on me at the end of the evening, and because I've been so attracted to him for so long—
and probably because a couple of glasses of
wine blurred what little common sense I've got
where he's concerned—what do I do? Say yes,
of course. Not only say yes but invite him back
here, and, of course, he wasn't called out during
the night. We both slept in, and the first person
he sees as he wanders downstairs is your father.'

Maggie gave Annie a despairing look.

'I've been here less than a week and I'm
bringing men home, so how do you think I felt
about facing Rod again? But somehow—mainly
thanks to your father's wonderful temperament
and social skills—we muddled past all that, your
father invites him back to dinner and I think
maybe it's going to be OK, and then what happens?'

'He flirts with me all through the meal,'
Annie said glumly, not knowing how to make
things right for Maggie. 'He's got to be
amoral—is that the word? Sleeps with women

but refuses to get emotionally involved. A no-strings playboy.'

Annie couldn't think of anything more to say, so she put her arm around Maggie and gave her a hug.

'What are you going to do?'

Another sigh came up from somewhere near Maggie's toes.

'Do?' she said, the word squeaky and the laugh that accompanied it just slightly hysterical. 'What can I do but go on as I did before? Pretend it never happened, that's what I have to do. If Phil Park can do it, so can I!'

She straightened out of Annie's embrace.

'In fact, I should have been stronger downstairs. Shouldn't have let him get to me. Come on, we'll go back down and brazen it out. No, better still, let's get dolled up and go out ourselves. Go clubbing.'

Never having enjoyed the dark atmosphere of nightclubs, Annie was underwhelmed by this idea, but this wasn't about the outing, it was about sisterhood and solidarity. She understood that part.

'I'm really tired,' she said, knowing she sounded pathetically weak but not willing to take sisterhood too far. 'Can we get dressed up and pretend to go out? Leave the house and drive across to the beach then come back in a little while when they've gone?'

Maggie looked a bit disappointed but in the end agreed that she was also tired. Another sigh, this one regretful.

'He really was the most wonderful lover,' she said softly, then she shook off this momentary weakness and headed for her bathroom, poking her head back out the door to add, 'Wear something that will knock both their socks off.'

Annie trudged down the short corridor to her room. She wasn't against knocking Alex's socks off, just upset he was here, because doing this, in the name of solidarity and sisterhood, would make it look as if she preferred an evening out with Maggie to spending some time with him.

Maybe it was for the best. If he decided she was a frivolous, uncaring pleasure-seeker he might lose all interest in her and she could put a stop to all the futile arguments going on in her head.

She opened her wardrobe doors and looked inside.

'Knock their socks off?'

She echoed Maggie's words with despair. There was nothing in her wardrobe that could squeeze, even by the smallest margin, into that description. During her time with Dennis she'd worn nothing but high-necked, long-sleeved sweaters or shirts, and when she'd finally reached Sydney and gone shopping for new clothes, habit had had her doing the same thing.

One dress—bought to wear to work functions she couldn't avoid—also had the requisite high neckline. But it was in the dark green colour she liked wearing, was well cut and the fine fabric clung to her figure like a second skin. She loved it and felt good in it—but it was hardly a sock-knocking-off creation.

It would have to do.

Maggie, in a bright red miniskirt, lacy top and shiny red boots, took one look at her and dragged her into her bedroom.

'I don't have any knock-their-socks off clothes,' Annie explained, not liking the note of apology in her voice. Here she was doing Maggie a favour and apologising for how she looked!

Maggie slid open her wardrobe and looked from it to Annie.

'You have black trousers or jeans?'

Maggie nodded.

'OK, slip into them, and put on this top. Black boots?'

Maggie shook her head and Annie rummaged through a collection of shoes that would had done Imelda Marcos proud, and produced a pair of pointy-toed black boots with heels so high Annie was sure she'd fall over in them.

She was about to protest when she remembered solidarity again—and how upset Maggie had been over Phil's behaviour!—so she took the top and boots and went glumly back to her room.

Maybe if she took long enough, their two visitors would have gone, but Maggie didn't let her dither, following her with a serious-looking make-up case.

'You can't go out without eye shadow,' she announced, waiting only until Annie had slipped off her dress and pulled on the top before sitting her down and applying various potions and powders to Annie's face.

Ten minutes later Maggie pronounced herself satisfied, though she added rather bitterly, 'Though why I'm making sure you look stunning when Phil already fancies you, I don't know.'

'He doesn't fancy me at all,' Annie assured her, wondering how any woman could wear a top cut so low without spending the entire evening blushing and tugging it upward. 'He just flirts with any woman not yet certified dead.'

She made her way cautiously downstairs, heart leaping around in her chest when she heard voices in the kitchen and knew her prayer that the visitors might have departed hadn't been answered.

The boots had to be two sizes too small, but all she had to do was get through the kitchen and out to the car, where she could kick them off.

'I'll go first,' Maggie said, when they reached the bottom. 'Now, the rule here is "never explain"! We'll just sashay through, say "goodnight, boys" and keep going.'

That suited Annie just fine, although she usually gave her father more particular information about her whereabouts.

'We'd better say where to,' she whispered to Maggie, who looked surprised, and then quite pleased.

'Good idea—that way they can follow us!'

'We're not really going there,' Annie reminded her, and Maggie looked disappointed.

'We're all dressed up—we may as well,' she said, and Maggie realised she should never had let thoughts of solidarity and sisterhood guide her path. If she was doing anything this evening, it should be with Alex.

No, it shouldn't!

Well, maybe not, but if she couldn't be with Alex she didn't want to be with anyone else.

Alex heard footsteps tapping towards the kitchen. High-heeled footsteps from the sound of them. He'd watched Maggie depart from the dinner table, then Annie follow, and wondered just what was going on.

Apart from Phil flirting with Annie all through dinner! What was happening there? Annie certainly hadn't encouraged him but, then, she hadn't singled him, Alex, out for attention either. She'd eaten her meal with desperate concentration, as if wishing she could be teleported to some other place.

The good thing was, her single-minded attack on the delicious meal had allowed him to study her—unobtrusively, he hoped. She wasn't the most beautiful woman he'd ever met, and she did very little to make the most of her striking eyes and neat, straight features. Not wanting to attract attention?

Male attention?

So why had she attracted his?

Why did he feel—and had felt from the beginning—that there was something special about this woman? That she was—or should be—his?

The tapping footsteps drew closer, and he had to revise all his assumptions about Annie not wanting to attract attention. Next to Maggie in her bright red miniskirt and red boots, Annie, all in black, should have been invisible, yet Alex was stunned by her beauty.

'We're off out,' Maggie said, grabbing Annie's arm and all but dragging her across the room.

'Not without an escort you're not,' Phil said, leaping to his feet so quickly his chair tipped over. 'Come on, Alex. We've got our pagers. You can't let these two beauties out on their own. Who knows who they'll pick up?'

Alex looked at Annie for guidance but found she was looking at Phil.

'Who knows?' she repeated in a voice so dry it scratched.

Then she looked at Alex, and he thought he detected a plea in her eyes, but was it a 'come along and save me' plea, or a plea that he stay out of whatever was going on?

That something was going on, he had no doubt. And that it affected Maggie more than Annie, he was also certain. Annie might look stunningly beautiful, but the way she held herself was reminiscent of paintings he'd seen of aristocratic women being dragged off to the guillotine. Whatever was going on, Annie was a far from willing participant, and this fact alone had him rising to his feet.

'I guess a little gallantry on a Saturday night wouldn't hurt,' he said. 'But I need to change out of trainers and we should go in my car anyway. You're not drinking, Phil, so you can drive.'

And all I have to do is manoeuvre Annie into the back seat and this might turn out OK after all!

He winked at Annie, but she didn't seem as delighted—or even as relieved—as he'd expected.

And now he'd missed his opportunity to start the manoeuvring, as Phil had moved closer to her and was ushering her towards the door.

Any moment now the situation would be lost.

Then Annie turned towards him—just a despairing glance his way—and the Galahad within him finally awoke.

'No way, Phil,' he said, elbowing his colleague aside. 'If we're making a foursome, then Annie's my date.'

He put his arm possessively around her waist—so small—and tried to draw her close, but he'd obviously misread the glance for she pushed away.

'No one's anyone's date,' she snapped. 'Maggie and I decided we wanted to go out. If you guys want to come that's fine, but you're tagging along, nothing more. Maggie and I might both meet our soul mates tonight, so we don't want our opportunities spoiled by you two behaving as if this is a date.'

If he'd been stunned before, he was doubly so this time, and though Annie now shot him a look that he *could* read as apologetic, he'd been wrong about reading the look she'd shot him just before, so he could easily be wrong again.

'Come on,' she was saying to Maggie, who looked as utterly miserable as someone dressed in red could possibly look, 'let's go.'

Annie hooked her arm through Maggie's and practically dragged her through the front door.

'You got us into this and now you're going to have to go through with it. And stop looking sorry for yourself,' she muttered fiercely. 'My feet are killing me in these boots, and on top of that I'm going to stretch them and have to fork out huge amounts of money to replace them for you.'

Maggie relaxed enough to give a very small giggle, but Annie had to continue to force her to move—out the front door and up the road towards Alex's house—the conversation of the two men following them.

'It's all backfired,' Maggie whispered.

'I know it has,' Annie told her. 'But who knows? Maybe something good will come out of it. Maybe you'll meet some gorgeous guy who makes you forget all about Phil.'

Maggie didn't seem to believe her but thinking about Maggie's problems, Annie decided, was better than considering where she now stood with Alex. Maybe after this performance he'd forget about this obsession he had for dating her, which would be the best thing for both of them, even if her heart ached at the thought and her mind chided her for the way she'd spoken to him earlier.

Alex had been too good to her—considerate, understanding, great kisser... Forget the kisses.

Anyway, it had been a terrible way to treat him when all he'd done had been to come to her rescue so she wouldn't have to keep avoiding Phil's hands. But Maggie would have been miserable with a situation where Phil was forced into being her date. She wanted Phil to want her for herself, not as someone to make up the numbers.

Annie tried to sort through the problem in her head. As Phil was driving, maybe she could slip into the back seat with Alex and whisper that she'd explain about it later.

Only she couldn't explain much—not without breaking Maggie's confidence!

Damn!

They'd reached Alex's house, and Minnie was yapping excitedly from behind the front door. She turned somersaults of delight at seeing Alex and Phil, then showed nearly as much excitement when she recognised Annie.

Annie bent and picked her up, and was letting the little dog nuzzle her chin when Maggie said, 'I'm glad she's black. That way people won't notice the dog hairs on my best top.'

Alex and Phil were on their way up the stairs to change, and Annie heard Alex's footsteps falter at the comment.

'Don't you like dogs?' she asked Maggie, who sighed for about the fortieth time that evening.

'I love them. I have one at home that I had to leave with my parents. I'm just feeling bitchy and you know why.'

Alex had disappeared but Annie sensed he'd heard at least part of the conversation. She hoped he'd heard enough to realise there were things going on here that were beyond her control.

Also beyond her control were the seating arrangements in the car, for Maggie took over, climbing into the back seat while Alex held the door, dragging Annie in behind her.

'Great date, this,' Phil said, glancing at a silent Alex in the seat beside him.

'It's not a date,' Maggie snapped. 'You two asked yourselves along on an outing, that's all!'

Annie decided silence was the best option—that way she shouldn't get herself into any more trouble. But she hadn't figured Alex's determination into the equation. They were no sooner inside the club, Maggie heading with some resolve towards the bar, than Alex caught Annie's arm and nodded towards the small dance floor where a few couples shuffled to the music of a four-piece group.

And being in his arms, dancing with him again, she was in more trouble than she could ever have imagined, because this felt like bliss. It felt as if this was how things were meant to be.

It felt like heaven…

'For all her finery, Maggie doesn't look happy.'

Thoughts of heaven vanished. Alex had only asked her to dance to question her. She wasn't surprised he wanted to know what was going on, so why had she thought this dance was something more?

Something special?

'She's not, but she'll get over it,' Annie said, then realised she sounded snappy. 'I assume,' she added, hoping that made her sound more sympathetic towards their colleague.

'I certainly hope so. I hate bad feelings between members of the team.'

You might have to put up with it, Annie thought as she became increasingly cross with him for pursuing the conversation and not enjoying the dance as she was.

For five years she'd had memories of being held in this man's arms—dancing with him—now here she was and he was grumbling about people not getting on at work.

Maybe if she edged a little closer...

'I've always thought Maggie fancied Phil, though why any woman would be interested in a man who flirts with every female on the planet I don't know.'

So much for moving closer!

'I think it's an inherited disposition in Phil's case. Apparently his father was a noted philanderer.'

Realising they were on different planes as far as mood was concerned, Annie reluctantly joined the conversation.

'Phil told you that? Boasted about his father's proclivities?'

'No, my mother told me.'

The evening, which had begun badly when Annie had come downstairs in her scruffy state, now deteriorated to the farcical stage.

'Your mother knew Phil's father?'

Alex laughed. 'Biblically, you mean?' he said, and laughed again. 'No, she read his autobiography. No, maybe it wasn't auto, maybe it was just a biography because if he'd written it, he might not have boasted about his sexual exploits—not an Englishman.'

'Phil's an Englishman and his behaviour doesn't indicate any delicacy where relationships with women are concerned,' Annie said, although she was more intrigued by Phil's father having had a biography written about him. 'Was he someone famous?' she asked. 'Phil's father?'

'More notorious, my mother said,' Alex explained. 'One of those upper-class Englishmen who had too much money and not enough to do with their time, so he played—all over the world, apparently. Drove fast cars and even faster boats and did daring, adventurous things, but in the end he must have got bored with playing and actually got interested in Antarctica and did a lot of the modern-day exploration down there.'

'Which wouldn't have brought him any closer to his children, one would think,' Annie said.

'No, it didn't,' Alex agreed, finally tightening his hold on Annie as if he'd realised they were dancing, not holding a conversation standing up. 'That's about the only thing Phil's ever said about his father—that he rarely saw him and barely knew him. Phil and his brother and sister grew up in the family home in the country, in the north somewhere, cared for by nannies and servants, while his mother grieved—Phil's word—for the husband who was gone but not dead.'

'That's so sad,' Annie said, and nestled closer to Alex's strong body.

His arms tightened a little more so he could hold her close, and finally she was reliving her dream, dancing with Alex, feeling as light as thistledown because of the magic of being in his arms.

'If I kiss you, am I breaking the "it's not a date" embargo?' he whispered against her hair a little later.

'Probably, but it doesn't matter—it's been lifted. I've done my duty to the sisterhood and from now on the night is mine.'

She knew Alex wouldn't have a clue what she was talking about, but she didn't care, allowing him to draw her into the darkest, most shadowed corner of the dance floor and bend his head to kiss her on the lips.

'Ah!'

She heard her own murmur of pleasure and relief, and imagined she heard a similar sound escape him, then they were kissing as if they'd just discovered how to, exploring their senses through lips alone.

'Not particularly good form, kissing on a dance floor,' a cool voice said, and Annie jerked away from Alex to see Phil, his arms around a blonde, dancing very close to where they stood.

'Where's Maggie?' she demanded, no doubt startling Alex with her vehemence. But if Maggie had seen Phil ask the blonde to dance, and had been left, deserted at the bar, who knew what she might do? Annie looked frantically around, but they were in a corner and she couldn't see the bar.

'Relax,' Phil said easily, nuzzling his lips to the blonde's neck and making Annie want to belt him. 'She's on the floor with some Neanderthal lifesaver type, dancing so close you couldn't slip a tissue between them.'

'Oh, dear,' Annie muttered to herself, as Phil steered his partner away from them. 'This isn't working out at all as it should have!'

'No?' Alex said, slipping his arm around her shoulders. 'I'd say it's working perfectly. Phil and Maggie are both above the age of consent— they both have partners for this dance if not for the night—so let's you and I slip out of here, get a cab home and kiss each other somewhere more private than this corner.'

Tempting though the offer was, Annie dithered. Kissing Alex somewhere private would be blissful, but deserting Maggie?

'I can't go,' she told Alex. 'At least, not until I've talked to Maggie. I can tell her the boots are killing me, which is true. I just didn't notice it while we were kissing.'

But Alex had already drawn away.

'What's going on, Annie?' he asked, and she knew he wanted a straight answer.

There was only one to give.

'I can't tell you,' she said, then watched him walk away, not back to the bar but past it and out of the door.

'It's for the best,' she told herself, making her own way back to the bar, where she found a stool, ordered a mineral water and rested her pinched and tortured feet, while fending off offers to dance, to drink, or to go home with various hopeful men.

CHAPTER ELEVEN

ANNIE woke very early on Sunday morning to a sense of great misgiving. She'd stayed on at the nightclub for another hour, then, because the offers from men she didn't know had been getting more drunken and insistent, she'd tried to persuade Maggie to leave.

But Maggie had been having a wonderful time and had been happy for Annie to go on home, though she had insisted on phoning a cab from the club to make sure Annie was safe.

Where Phil had disappeared to, neither of them knew, though Annie sensed he was still somewhere around—no doubt with the blonde and her friends.

Where things now stood, with Phil and Maggie or with herself and Alex, she had no idea, but she'd been worrying more about the Carters during the night and regretted not asking Alex about the latest news on their decision.

One way to find out. She'd pull on some clothes and go up to the hospital.

Mrs Carter was in Amy's room, and Annie marvelled at the woman's patience and dedication as she sat beside her failing daughter, talking softly to her and rubbing one finger across the little girl's skin. Up and down her arm, around drip tubes and monitor wires, down her cheek, across her head.

If loving touch could heal, Amy would be better.

Annie sidled into the room and was greeted with a smile.

'Did Dr Attwood talk to you yesterday?' she asked quietly.

Amy's mother nodded.

'He's a wonderful man—stayed with us all morning and some of the afternoon as well.'

No wonder Alex hadn't wanted to stay at the club! Annie thought, then Mrs Carter was talking again.

'He talked us through all the pros and cons and let us ask questions, and just sat because he said the more we thought about things, the more questions we'd come up with. And we did.'

Realising the woman was so much more relaxed than when Annie had last seen her, Annie guessed the family had reached some kind of decision and were happy with it.

Should she ask?

Was it her place?

She'd need to know, but Alex would eventually fill her in.

She was still mentally debating her position when Amy's mother continued.

'We decided while she's still stable—and Dr Attwood says she is. He showed us how the monitors tell him things, and said her condition wasn't deteriorating. He said sometimes babies get so sick with other things they can't do a transplant, but Amy's not like that so that's why we decided.'

Mrs Carter gave a little laugh.

'I still didn't tell you, did I? We're going to wait. He said to take each day as it comes and not to hope too hard, but to believe that if Amy's well enough for them to do a transplant when one becomes available, we'll go ahead. If she starts to slip or gets an infection or we feel she's suffering, we'll think again and maybe turn off the machines supporting her.'

Annie reached for the woman's free hand and gave it a squeeze. She was too choked up to speak, knowing just how hard this decision had been. Yet Mrs Carter was far more settled now than she'd been the previous morning after Annie had spent the night with her.

All because of Alex who, no doubt in his precise way, had made it all sound so rational and easy, divorcing the huge emotional content of the decision from the medical one and letting Amy's parents see a way through their dilemma.

'Have you slept at all?' Annie asked when she'd swallowed her own emotional reaction. 'I could sit with Amy if you like.'

Mrs Carter turned to her with a smile.

'I slept all night. Bill sat with Amy and he's gone off to sleep now. We're so thankful for the accommodation provided by organisations so we can stay close to our darling all the time.'

Annie chuckled, genuinely delighted to see the woman so positive. Annie had known from the first operation she'd seen him perform that Alex could work miracles inside the chests of tiny babies, but apparently he was just as good with miracles outside the theatre, too.

She was still smiling as she made her way to the office, thinking she'd catch up on some paperwork while she was there, but she was barely through the door when her pager chirped and her heart accelerated.

As unit manager, she was the one who would receive first news of an available heart, and though, on another day, a page might mean Becky contacting her from the office, on a Sunday the sound brought hope.

She knew by heart the plan Alex had given her. She had to find out the details, organise a retrieval flight, have planes and ambulances for the retrieval team standing by at each end of the journey. Or just an ambulance on alert, if the heart was in the city. A member of the surgical team, Phil preferably, would go with either Kurt or a nurse on the retrieval flight.

Annie ticked off this information as she dialled the number. It *was* the donor programme co-ordinator. A heart that might be suitable for Amy had become available in Brisbane. Did they want it?

'Yes,' Annie said, and got contact details of the hospital and attending paediatrician so Alex could talk direct to him. She paged Alex, then phoned the number she had for the Flying Marvels, a group of men and women who owned their own planes and volunteered to fly sick children to the city for treatment. They'd been used before for organ retrieval flights, and Annie was delighted when the man she spoke to said he could organise a flight to Brisbane and back and could have a plane and pilot waiting at the airport within forty minutes. Annie told him she'd phone him back to confirm it as soon as possible.

Alex phoned and once again Annie explained, giving him the Brisbane number and telling him she had a plane standing by.

'Who do you want to go?' she asked him, and he didn't hesitate.

'Phil—I'll wake him—and Kurt if you can get hold of him. He knows how to bring it back. But if you can't get hold of him, get Rachel—she's done retrievals before.'

'They both have pagers. I'll get one of them,' Annie assured him.

Alex hung up before she could ask if she should speak to the Carters or wait for him. Theirs would be the final decision—whether to put Amy through another operation, knowing that transplants could fail.

Annie looked at her hands and saw they were shaking, but there was so much still to do—people to call, arrangements to be confirmed.

Alex came into the office half an hour later, and Annie was able to tell him everyone was standing by.

'I'll talk to the Carters,' he said, and left the room, returning five minutes later.

'We're on,' he said. 'Can you give me a time frame for retrieval?'

'One hour and twenty minutes to Brisbane in the light plane, same for return trip, though one way is usually shorter than the other because of wind factors. Ambulance from here to the airfield, Sunday morning and not much traffic, twenty-five minutes, in Brisbane fifteen minutes. How long does Phil need?'

Alex looked at the ceiling for a moment.

'Thirty—maybe forty minutes.'

Annie was on the phone as they had this conversation, first confirming with the donor organisation that, yes, they'd take the heart, then speaking to the Flying Marvels man, getting details of where the team should meet the pilot and explaining where they were going.

'We have a cooler?'

Annie, dialling Kurt's number, looked up.

'A cooler?'

Alex made a gesture with his hands, outlining the shape of a small box.

'For drinks!'

And it dawned on Annie that in this day and age of such sophisticated medical technology, they carried hearts for transplant around in a drinks cooler.

'Pathology has heaps of them,' she said, then told Kurt that Phil would collect him in twenty minutes. Alex disappeared and she phoned the ambulance, asking them to pick up Phil from the hospital and to be standing by for a return trip from the airport in a little over three hours.

Alex returned with a cooler and Phil. Annie joined them and the three walked together to the ambulance bay. Not running, but certainly striding out as suddenly every minute counted.

'That's why we go by ambulance,' Alex said to her as the vehicle sped away, siren wailing. 'Whatever minutes we save are minutes we can add to Amy's life.'

He slid an arm around Annie's shoulders and led her back inside, and for a moment she thought he was going to talk about the previous evening.

Silly thought. The arm was nothing more than a teamly gesture—his mind was totally involved with what lay ahead.

'I'll need Rachel, and if you can get that male nurse—'

'Ned?' Annie suggested, and Alex nodded.

'That's the one, and Maggie. No hurry, but I'll open Amy up as soon as we know the plane has landed back here in Sydney. It's all a matter of timing now.'

Annie made her way back to the office, ready to field phone calls if anything went wrong. All the team had pagers, the flight people had her number, the hospital in Brisbane had her number. What could go wrong? The weather was perfect, flying conditions would be great.

Alex came in and dropped a piece of paper on her desk.

'That's the number of the sister on duty at the PICU in Brisbane. Could you phone her and get some more details on the baby?'

Annie looked up at him, knowing she was frowning.

'Didn't you do that when you spoke to the paediatrician?'

'I asked medical questions, Annie,' Alex said gently. 'We don't need to know names and addresses—in fact, confidentiality is key in these cases—but Amy's family will ask questions about the donor, and if we can answer them, everyone will feel more at ease.'

Annie knew what he was saying must be true because Alex had been involved in these situations before, but in this position would she want to know more about a baby that had died to give her child life?

She wasn't sure and her uncertainty must have showed for Alex leaned across the desk and touched her lightly on the shoulder.

'Believe me,' he said, 'the questions will come. Maybe not right away, but soon, and it's best for us to be prepared.'

He sat down in the chair across the desk from her, and she could see the understanding in his eyes. Understanding that she was still coming to grips with the situation. Oh, she'd coped with the physical side of it, organising and arranging, but emotionally? Yes, she was at a loss.

'Knowing a little about the donor makes it more personal—which you'd think might be a bad thing, but it isn't. It makes it less like a shopping trip—I'll take those shoes, and if you have a very small heart, I'd like one of them as well.'

Alex smiled, but Annie felt more like crying, grieving for the owner of that very small heart, and for the owner's parents and siblings, and all the relations.

She blinked away a tear, and said, 'OK, I'll take your word for it and find out more, but I think I'd prefer the shopping trip. That way I could pretend it was just a heart, not something that had once been part of a living, breathing baby.'

'No, you couldn't,' Alex argued. 'You might be able to pretend to others, but inside yourself you'd know the truth. You're too courageous for pretence to be part of your life.'

Annie looked at him and shook her head, knowing they were no longer talking about the baby but about her own life. Had Alex guessed it was all pretence, that he was saying this? Was he pushing her to be honest with him?

Heaven knew, she wanted to, but the thought that in doing so she might put him within reach of even the remotest possibility of danger had made her hold her tongue.

She shook her head, and said sadly, 'No, Alex, that's wrong. My entire adult life seems to have been about pretence. You're so open and honest—with parents, staff, everyone—that you can't imagine that other people aren't.'

Alex heard the words, even took them in, but looking at Annie—knowing what he did of her—he couldn't accept what she was saying. Annie and deceit? The equation didn't gel.

'We'll talk later,' he said, more determined than ever to find out what lay behind some of the things Annie had said.

He needed to find out what lay behind last night's outing, too. That it was something to do with Maggie, he knew—but what? And why had Annie not come home with him?

That was the question that had tormented him during his cab ride home, but once there he'd put the entire evening into the 'too hard basket' and had gone straight to bed. He'd had two hours' sleep in the past thirty-six and had needed to catch up. Fortunately for him—and Amy—he did sleep well.

Maggie was in Amy's room when he returned there, taking blood for testing and making notes to herself about the medications Amy had been on since the operation.

She followed Alex out and they discussed what would happen in Theatre and the drugs they'd need for different stages of the operation. Amy's blood would be cooled to minimise organ damage during the changeover, and she'd need drugs to thin her blood while she was on the bypass machine. Once the new heart was in place, a lot of the actions of the drugs would have to be reversed. It was important to get blood into the coronary arteries as soon as possible so they could feed the muscle of the new heart.

So many details—so much to anticipate. If this went wrong, what would they need? If that happened, did they have the equipment on hand to make it right?

'Flight's landed in Brisbane and the boys are on their way to the hospital,' Annie reported, poking her head around the door of the theatre anteroom where Maggie and Alex were talking.

'Keep us posted,' Alex told her, then Rachel and Ned arrived, and Alex included them in the discussion they were having, explaining the operation step by step, though he knew Rachel had been through this with him before.

'What theatre staff do we have?' Rachel asked, and Alex shook his head.

'Don't know, but for sure Annie's dug up the best she can find.'

'Blood?'

'Already on hand,' Maggie told Ned.

'So, you guys set up, I'm going to phone a friend. I stood in as a spare pair of hands for him on Friday night, now I'll wreck his weekend by asking him to do the same for me.'

He phoned from the anteroom, and when his colleague agreed to come, Alex felt excitement begin to build within him. A lot of the operations he did on children were more complex and risky than a heart transplant, but this was life-giving.

'Aren't all of them life-giving?' Annie asked, coming in a little later to tell him the plane was in the air on the return flight.

'Yes,' he agreed, 'insofar as the child could die if he or she isn't operated on, but they're different somehow.'

Annie wasn't sure she understood, but she nodded anyway, then was surprised when Alex put his arms around her and drew her close.

'You've found out more about the other baby,' he said gently—a statement, not a question.

She nodded against his shoulder.

'We didn't make that baby die, or even will its death, Annie,' Alex continued, 'but through the sadness of his death, we can offer hope for Amy. Can you not find some solace in that?'

'I suppose so,' she said, her voice muffled by his shirt. 'In fact, I know so, but just not yet.'

He kissed her lightly on the top of her head, and she knew it was a signal for her to leave the comfort of his arms. It was work time and every second counted.

Annie went back to her office. She ran through the procedure schedule Alex had given her when the unit had first opened. Every item had been ticked off. Pathologists were on standby, drugs available, extra staff on hand in case the operation took longer than expected and the special care unit staff primed for what to expect when Amy returned to them.

Which left the Carters, but Annie, knowing phone calls could be coming in, couldn't leave the office to talk to them. Once Amy was in Theatre, she could sit with them, and though part of her really wanted to see this operation, another part of her felt she would be more useful waiting with the parents.

Alex phoned as she made this decision. 'We're taking Amy into Theatre now,' he said, 'so when you hear anything, let us know in there.'

Annie was about to hang up when Alex added, 'Aren't you going to wish us luck?'

'You don't need luck—you're the best there is,' she told him, though she did add a soft 'Good luck!' before she put the phone down.

Now all she could do was sit and will the plane to land and the ambulance to make good time to the hospital. Once there, Phil and Kurt would have to scrub before taking their places in Theatre—Kurt already had a stand-in, a perfusionist from Children's, in Theatre, ready to operate the machine as soon as Amy was anaesthetised.

Looking back later, it seemed to Annie that everything had happened at once. The phone had rung to say the plane had come in and the ambulance was already on its way back to the hospital. The surgeon from Children's had arrived and Annie had taken him through to Theatre, then Phil and Kurt had arrived back, Phil holding the cooler with the heart as casually as he might have taken some cans of beer to a football game. Annie had watched him slide it through the theatre door, calling to Alex, 'It's just the best little heart. Behaved beautifully as we took it out. Be with you all shortly.'

Then he went to change and Annie sought out the Carters, sitting tensely in the family room off the special care unit.

'It's here?' they asked in unison, and Annie nodded, then Mrs Carter reached out for her hand.

'Tell me this is the right thing to do,' she pleaded, and Annie led her back to the settee and sat her down, sitting beside her and putting her arm around her shoulders.

'It seems to me,' she said carefully, 'that this is how things were meant to be. I mean, you'd decided to wait and see what happened—whether a heart became available while Amy was still relatively stable. The chances were so small really. I know Alex told you that. Yet it happened, and so quickly, and everything else fell into place, so don't you have to think it was meant to be?'

Mrs Carter considered this for a moment, then she nodded, while her husband, holding tightly to her hand now she was sitting down again, said, 'Makes you believe there's someone or something on our side. We wondered, when Amy was born with so much wrong and was so sick, whether it was our fault this had happened. But it's fate, isn't it? It's all about fate!'

He put his arm around his wife and Annie moved away, shifting to the armchair so the pair could share some physical comfort on the settee.

It seemed an interminable time but finally the door opened and Alex came in. He looked exhausted and Annie feared the worst, but he summoned up a smile for the Carters and said, 'All well so far. Her new heart is beating beautifully.'

They rose as one, Mr Carter gripping Alex's hand, Mrs Carter throwing herself against him and hugging him tightly.

Alex waited a moment, then said, 'She's not out of the woods yet, remember. Her body could reject it, or she could react badly to the drugs we have to give her to guard against rejection. Then there are other organs that might have been affected by the length of time she was on bypass.'

Annie listened, amazed as ever that Alex could list so many negatives yet still keep hope alive in his listeners. It wasn't that he told anything but the plain, unvarnished truth, yet people heard it with hope in their hearts and trusted him enough to believe those bad things wouldn't happen.

She studied him, wondering how the faith others had in him must affect him, physically and emotionally, when the bad things he spoke of did happen. For a moment superstition replaced faith and fate, and she crossed her fingers. Not for Amy, she prayed silently. Don't let the bad things happen for her.

Alex left the room but Annie lingered in case the Carters wanted to ask questions, but they were so excited and delighted she might as well not have been there so she walked back to the office where Alex was slumped at his desk.

'What's wrong?' she demanded, frightened by this sight of a dejected Alex. 'Did things not go as well as you made out?'

He lifted his head and gave her a tired smile.

'Afterburn!' he said. 'At least, that's what I call it. It's a kind of exhaustion that comes with the let-down of tension when an op like that is done. I always feel totally wrung out. Phil's different, he gets a high, and I understand that because I feel like that after a good switch, or something regular, but for some reason I can't feel that euphoria after a transplant. For all my brave words to you and to the Carters, I still feel as if I'm meddling with fate, and on some atavistic level it scares the hell out of me.'

'Oh, Alex,' Annie said gently, walking towards him so she could perch on the desk and lean forward to massage his shoulders and neck, 'you give so much confidence, and talk such common sense to other people, can't you spare some for yourself?'

He smiled again and took her hand, resting it against her cheek.

'Later, I'll be able to,' he promised, 'especially if Amy pulls through the next few days. If that happens, I'll take it as a sign that fate didn't mind me meddling. Maybe even approved of it.'

He pressed a kiss into her palm, then gave her back her hand, and she knew he needed to be alone to work through his let-down in the way that best suited him.

Other members of the team drifted in, most of them, as Alex had foretold, on a high.

'Come on, late lunch in the canteen. The tab's on me,' Phil said, and even Alex stood up and joined the others trooping out. He turned back and waved to Annie, but she shook her head. Phil had put his arm around Maggie as he'd made the suggestion, and there was no way she was going to rain on whatever small parade Maggie might be enjoying.

'I've some phone calls to make. I told the Flying Marvels I'd let them know how things went, and I need to call a few other people who've been involved.'

Alex didn't argue but followed the others out, and though Annie told herself he had to go because the lunch would serve as a debrief after the operation, she was still disappointed.

'Stupidly disappointed!' she muttered to herself. 'Get over it!'

She didn't get over it, but she did get through the day, and then the week, and even into the next week. Amy had thrown up every complication Alex had predicted and then some, and he'd been all but living at the hospital, returning home at weird times to grab clean clothes but otherwise making the on-duty room off the special care unit his home.

Annie told herself this was good because, although she still saw him any number of times a day, and still had regular conferences with him over his consulting appointments and operating programme, work was always on both their minds, if not to the exclusion of all else, at least blotting out most of the manifestations of their attraction. The team might be operating normally, but every member of it was emotionally caught up in Amy's roller-coaster ride.

'Her condition's turned,' Alex finally announced the following Thursday. He'd called the team together, and Annie had found herself hoping it wasn't to say he was going to put Amy back on the list for a transplant.

His words elicited a rough cheer from the group and Alex smiled, his tired, drawn face lightening so imperceptibly that Annie felt her heart tug with pity for him.

'Days off all round! We've no ops scheduled for tomorrow so, the medical team, you're off for three days—four if Annie can juggle Monday's list and fit the ops in later in the week. Nursing staff, again, see Annie. We've enough experienced people who've been working with our patients on the ward to maybe bump some of them to the PICU and give you lot from there a few days off as well.'

He turned expectantly to Annie.

'Annie?'

She wasn't sure she had *that* many nurses at her disposal, but it was so good to see Alex starting to relax that she smiled at him and said, 'Can do, boss!'

She'd do it, even if it meant taking a nursing shift herself. The PICU was still a very familiar environment to her.

Alex went on to detail why he felt Amy was showing more stable improvement and why he didn't expect her condition to deteriorate again.

then ran through what they'd be doing the following week and sent everyone home.

Everyone but Annie, who had to check the nursing rosters and see how she could juggle staff, and also to see the intensivist on duty at the PICU—how much easier to call it that as Alex and Phil did, than the special care unit—and make sure he knew the surgeons wouldn't be quite as available to him in emergencies as they had been twenty-four hours a day since Amy's operation.

She was pencilling her name into the altered nursing roster—she could work Saturday and Sunday nights—when Alex walked into the office, a bunch of flowers in his hand and a much better smile on his face.

'These are for the best unit manager in the country, and I've more ordered for my best girl. They'll be waiting for you at a little cabin in the mountains where I'm taking you first thing tomorrow.'

CHAPTER TWELVE

ALEX looked at his unit manager and best girl and wondered why flowers and promises of a weekend escape had made her look so unhappy.

He put the flowers on the desk between them and sat down across from her.

It was the cabin idea—it had to be. He'd got so carried away with advancing their relationship with a weekend away, he hadn't considered Annie's feelings.

'It's a two-bedroom cabin, Annie. I won't rush you into anything.'

She smiled but it was such a sad effort he felt his heart sink.

'A cabin in the mountains sounds blissful,' she said, then she pushed a piece of paper across the desk towards him and pointed to a couple of squares. 'But you were right about our special nursing staff being due a few days off, and the only way I can work it for them is by doing a couple of shifts myself.'

'Nursing?'

The idea was bizarre.

'I am a nurse, and I'm a good one,' she reminded him, 'and honestly, Alex, the very last thing I expected was for you to come up with the idea of a weekend away. The last few weeks—'

'We haven't had any personal time,' he finished for her. 'But you know why that's happened. We haven't had a spare moment.'

She reached out and took his hand, removing the pen he'd been using to doodle triangles around her name on the roster.

'That isn't what I was going to say,' she told him. 'I was going to say I thought maybe you'd accepted there couldn't be anything between us.'

Alex could feel anger building inside him. For a moment he thought about fighting it but, damn it all, there was something special between him and Annie and no way was he going to let her hang-ups destroy that.

'Because of some rubbish about your past? About pretence? Do you think I care what happened in your marriage? Do you think I care that you might not be who you say you are? I know *you*, the person. That's who I fell in love with—not with a name, whether it's Annie Talbot or Rowena Drake.'

He knew immediately he'd made a mistake, but he hadn't counted on Annie's reaction. Sheet-white—there was no other way to describe her colour. Alex leapt to his feet and rushed around to grab her before she fainted. He eased her head down onto the desk and knelt beside her.

'Annie, it was just a guess—well, more than a guess because I went through the congress lists five years ago to try to work it out. It doesn't matter—that's what I was trying to say. I don't give two hoots who you are because it's a person I love, not a name.'

She lifted her head and looked at him, and he cursed himself because he knew he was responsible for the shadows of fear he saw in her eyes.

'Does anyone—?' she began, but the ringing of the phone cut her off. She lifted the receiver, said her name and listened, then sighed and shook her head.

'It's OK, Dad, Alex is here. We'll come right home and drive out together to pick them up.'

'Pick who up?' Alex asked, as Annie stood up, still pale but obviously in control of herself now.

'Henry and Minnie. Apparently Mayarma was knocked down by a car on her way home from the park and, although she's not badly injured, she was taken to hospital. The dogs were collected by the council dog-catcher and Dad's just had a phone call from the pound to ask if we could, please, collect our dogs.'

Alex knew Annie was worrying about Henry now, but he guessed she was also pleased that this small crisis had diverted them from the conversation they'd been having.

So much for plans for the weekend! he thought grimly, following her out of the office then out of the hospital.

'We could take my car,' he suggested when they were close to his place.

'Henry in your precious BMW? I don't think so. But I've got my car keys so we can cut through your place and down the lane to my garage. Do you want to come or will I collect Minnie for you as well? There'll be a fine to pay, even though it was an unavoidable circumstance.'

'I'll come with you,' Alex insisted, taking her arm as they walked through his gate, wondering if maybe they were past whatever had shocked her earlier. Wondering also if they could get another nurse to take Annie's place on that damn roster.

Annie drove, refusing to think of anything but Henry. Well, part of her mind was on Alex's revelation that he knew her real name, and that part was mentally arguing that it couldn't possibly hurt, but most of her mind was on Henry and how he was handling incarceration.

'I'd hate anything to happen to Henry.' She blurted out the words, only realising, once they were said, that more of her mind than she'd thought must still be on Rowena Drake.

And Alex was looking at her strangely, so something of her sudden surge of fear must have sounded in her words.

'They don't shoot dogs in the pound, you know. Well, not in pounds back home. They give the owners time to come pick them up. Plenty of time. More than a few hours.'

But Annie hardly heard the last sentences, the 'they don't shoot dogs' hammering so loudly in her ears it blotted out everything else.

'Why would you say that?' she whispered, driving up the track that led to the animal shelter and stopping the car so she could turn and look at Alex.

He was frowning at her.

'About having time to pick up your dog?'

Annie shook her head. She could feel her lips trembling.

'About shooting dogs.'

The words were little more than a murmur carried on a halting breath of air, but Annie was once again sheet-white. Alex leaned towards her and drew her close.

'I'm sorry. It was a figure of speech. Nothing more. A joke, Annie, if in poor taste.'

He held her close and kissed her head, his hands stroking her back, knowing he had to offer what comfort he could, knowing also that there was more than just a name change in Annie Talbot's past.

'OK,' he said, when the tremors in her body had eased and she was relaxed against him. 'Let's get these dogs then go back to my place or your place or somewhere private and have a long talk about all of this, because no matter who you are, I love you, and there's no way you're going to push me out of your life.'

Annie lifted her head and looked at him. He read surprise, and hope, and what he thought might even be love in her eyes.

'Oh, Alex!' she whispered, then she kissed him on the lips.

Kiss-deprived for so long, he drank in the taste of her, but she moved away.

'The pound will close. They were staying open an extra hour to try to sort out Mayarma's dogs, but the hour must be almost up.'

She moved away from him, opening the door on her side and climbing out. He joined her and put his arm around her as they walked towards the office.

'Henry Talbot,' Annie said, when asked for the dog's name. 'He's a Rottweiler.'

'Ah, Henry, yes,' the woman behind the desk said. 'You own the little spoodle, too. You really should change the Melbourne address on her tag.'

'The spoodle's not mine,' Annie said. 'She belongs to Alex.'

She turned to indicate Alex, who gave the woman a brave smile.

'Oh,' the woman said. 'We thought they must belong to the same owner. We couldn't separate them.'

'Henry's protective of her,' Annie explained, and Alex realised that's exactly how he felt towards Annie. He loved her, he was certain of that, but the protective issue was something new. He'd never felt like this about any other woman—and had always believed protection was associated with emotional dependency. Now here he was, *wanting* Annie to be emotionally dependent on him.

To a certain degree!

'It's forty dollars.'

The way Annie said the words suggested she was repeating them, but they still didn't make sense to Alex.

'For the fine,' the woman explained. 'I know it sounds silly when they were brought in because the walker had an accident, but we have to follow the rules.'

Alex caught up with the conversation and paid Minnie's fine, then, with the woman leading the way, they walked around to the wire runs at the back of the office building.

Henry's bulk made him immediately obvious, but his demeanour was in such contrast to Minnie's delighted hysteria when she saw her rescuers that Alex had to laugh.

'He's got his ''what took you so long'' look on his face,' Annie said, and Alex put his arm around her shoulders.

'If he had a wristwatch, he'd be looking at it,' he said, enjoying both dogs' behaviour and pleased they had the dogs to talk about and laugh about so some of the tension of the previous conversation could drain away.

Enough tension for him to once again raise the subject of a weekend away?

They talked of the dogs most of the way home, and then, because he was anxious to know if it might be possible, Alex gambled.

'We still haven't talked about the weekend,' he said.

Annie glanced his way then concentrated on turning into their back lane. There'd be other weekends for both of them, she was suddenly sure of it, but she wanted to let Alex down gently.

'Why don't you come home with me and we'll talk about it?' she said, then, knowing it was time, she added, 'We can talk about a lot of things.'

'Great, but can we stop at my place? I'll drop Minnie home. I think she's a little dog who's had enough excitement for one day.'

He indicated the scrap of black curls sleeping soundly on his knee.

Annie pulled up outside his back gate, and Alex turned and kissed her on the lips.

'You go on home. I'll feed Minnie and see she's got fresh water, then walk down.'

'Come the back way—we'll be in the kitchen,' Annie said, and with the feel of his kiss still lingering on her lips she drove slowly the short distance to her home.

'Home again, boy,' she said to Henry as she slid out of the car, but poor Henry wasn't released as easily. The clip on the short lead that held him to a safety harness in the back seat was stiff, and she fumbled with it for a few minutes before finally getting it free. She could have released it from Henry's collar, but he had the idea the back lane was a place of dog magic and took off down it whenever he had the chance, so she always kept the lead on until they were well inside the yard.

'You've had your burst of freedom for today,' she reminded him, holding him in check as they came out the garage door. She saw her father waiting in his wheelchair in the doorway, a shadowy figure she thought might be Phil in the kitchen behind him.

'Why haven't you got the kitchen light on?' she called, then the world went mad. The shadowy figure yelled something so unbelievable she couldn't take it in, her father hurtled towards her in the chair, Henry started barking furiously and leaping against his lead so it was all she could do to hold him. Then Alex came flying over the fence between her place and next door, grabbed her father's wheelchair and sent it spinning off the path.

Annie was still trying to assimilate this and come to grips with who was in the doorway when shots rang out and Henry collapsed, dragging her down on top of him, her body deathly cold, her mind wondering how Dennis could possibly have found them.

Alex raced to Annie and knelt over her, easing her off Henry's body but unable to tell which blood was hers and which was Henry's. Annie had a pulse, and from the way blood was spurting from the dog, he, too was alive. Then Rod was there.

'He's dead—Dennis. Shot himself. And an ambulance is on the way—I had my mobile with me. Annie?'

Rod's voice shook as he asked the question.

'She's going to be OK,' Alex told him, and heard a quaver in his own voice. 'I think Henry took the first bullet. Annie's only wound seems to be high up in her shoulder. Maybe lung involvement, but even that's not too bad if they get her straight to A and E.'

He ripped off his shirt, then tore it to strips with his teeth and was binding a pad over the bleeding wound as he spoke. Annie was unconscious, but his heart kept telling him she'd make it. *Had* to make it.

Rod was talking to him again—something about the dog—and Alex forced his attention away from Annie's milk-white face to concentrate on what Rod was saying.

'Have to get him to the vet. Take Annie's car, there's a spare set of keys beside the phone. The vet's number's there as well.'

'I can't leave her to take the dog to the vet,' Alex said. Although he knew there was nothing more he could do for Annie here, there was no way he was moving from her side.

Then Rod grasped his shoulder and tugged at him so Alex had to turn.

'Listen to me,' he roared. 'You get that dog to the vet and you damn well make sure you save him. Get a heart transplant for him if necessary, but I'm telling you, if you've a scrap of feeling for Annie you'll keep that dog alive.'

He paused, then in a ragged voice muttered, 'She didn't tell me for a long time after she came home, but he shot her other dog. The only damn friend she had in America.'

And Alex understood. He turned Henry gently, found the wound and used the rest of his shirt to make a pad which he pushed into place. Nothing to hold it there until Rod passed him his belt.

With the bleeding stopped, Alex paused only long enough to touch Annie's cheek then sprinted to the house, found the phone, the vet's number and Annie's keys, got directions on how to get to the surgery and returned to find the ambulancemen already bent over Annie.

'Give me a hand with the dog,' he said to one of them. 'It's important he lives.'

'I'll say it is,' another voice said, and Alex turned to find a policeman standing there. 'Damn monster, shooting at a harmless dog.'

It took three of them to lift Henry into the back of Annie's car, then the policeman asked which vet, and when Alex told him, the man said, 'Follow me.'

He went out to the back lane where a motor-bike leaned against the fence, strapped on his helmet, and when Alex started Annie's car the policeman took off, siren wailing, leading Alex on a hectic race through the streets to the vet's surgery.

*　　*　　*

'Dogs were used a lot for experimental heart surgery,' Alex said three hours later, sinking into a chair beside Rod, who was keeping vigil at Annie's bedside.

Rod turned towards him and nodded, understanding that Alex had stayed for the operation on Henry.

'He's all right?' Rod asked.

'He will be,' Alex told him. 'He'd lost a lot of blood and the bullet has damaged his right shoulder joint. It'll be a while before he can move freely again and he'll probably develop arthritis in the joint.'

'Bastard!' Rod muttered, then he reached out and touched his daughter's cheek.

She lay so still Alex had wondered if she'd slipped back into unconsciousness, but the anaesthetist he'd spoken to had told him she'd come out of the anaesthetic well, and this was just a deep, healing sleep.

'She never told me a thing,' Rod continued. 'Not even about the dog. Not till a long time after she came home. The night she left him— walked out of that fancy hotel in the middle of nowhere and walked all the way to the local police station—she asked the man on duty to phone me, and when he put her on the phone, she just said, ''He hits me, Dad.'' I thought my heart would burst with anger, that she'd been all the way over there and had been putting up with that kind of abuse. I'd have killed him myself if he'd been near. It was the kind of thing I'd seen time and time again in my working life, but for it to be happening to my own daughter…'

Rod paused as if the magnitude of his thoughts was too great to put into words. Alex understood, for his own insides were knotted with rage—made worse because it was futile to rage over something in the past.

'The best thing—apart from her finally leaving the sod—was that she found the right person to talk to in Jed McCabe. That's the policeman, and when you go back home, you might visit him for me and shake his hand. That Jed and his wife, they believed her, you see. Not all coppers do, and most hate domestics more than murder. But Jed had seen domestic violence firsthand in his wife's family and he brought his wife straight in. She took Annie somewhere private and made her take off her clothes, and she took pictures so there'd be proof if there was trouble. The bastard never touched her face, and hadn't hit her at the hotel, but old bruises were still there—yellow and purple, and thick places on her chest where broken ribs had healed. Anyway, Jed's wife, she got in touch with some mob over there who look after women like Annie—see, I call her that all the time now, that's who she is to me—and this mob made all the arrangements for her to start a new life.'

Rod's voice cracked again, but he steadied himself.

'I sent money—to Jed—and a month later Annie Talbot flew into Sydney. And you know what, Dennis never once contacted me—not in that month while I was at home. Two days after she phoned, a private investigator called me, and they've come ever since. Dennis never gave up. For five years the people he pays have been visiting and phoning our family back in West Australia, but we cut ourselves off from everyone. That was hard on Annie, losing her cousins and especially her gran, who'd helped to bring her up.'

Alex swallowed a lump that had made its way into his throat and shook his head in disbelief at what human beings could do to each other. He thought of the dead body he'd done no more than glance at in the doorway of Annie's house, and at the same moment heard Rod's question.

'What I can't understand is how the devil he found us now. After five years. What brought him here of all places? Right to our house?'

Alex felt his insides turn to lead, a sinking feeling spreading through his body. Two weeks ago he'd asked his old administrator to find out what she could about Dennis Drake, and although she hadn't come up with much more than his current employment at a hospital in San Diego, Alex knew for certain that somehow Dennis had found out about the questions.

And once he'd known who was enquiring, it would be an easy step to find out where he, Alex, was working. Take time off, fly out to Sydney—

Alex's reconstruction stopped dead at that point, as another thought demanded attention. In the canteen—the whole group had been there— and, like a familiar face glimpsed in a crowd, Alex had noticed someone he'd thought he knew, or recognised from somewhere—but they'd all been talking and he'd thought no more about it.

Had Dennis Drake been in the canteen?

Where better to see most of the workers in the hospital than where they ate?

So, he'd recognised Alex...

'Excuse me,' he said to Rod, knowing he'd be tortured about this until he found out.

He went down to the front desk, but the night staff didn't know if anyone had been asking for him.

'Have you checked your pigeonhole?' one woman asked, and though he doubted Dennis Drake would have left him a message, he did check.

No note, but why would there be?

He was making his way back to Annie's room when he passed one of the sisters from the PICU in civvies, as if she'd already left the hospital and come back for something.

'Did a cardiologist from San Diego catch up with you?' she asked. 'He came by this after-noon and was really interested in the unit. Says they need one where he works over there. He took that little newsletter Becky did when the unit started—the one with the photo of all the staff.'

Somehow Alex found the strength to thank her, but this confirmation that he had indeed led Dennis Drake to Annie had shattered him. He remembered Annie protesting when Becky had taken the photo, but they'd all insisted she be included. Her name, Annie Talbot, was under her photo—all the staff were mentioned by name—and Alex knew Dennis would only have to flash his credentials and say he was an old friend for someone on the admin staff to break the rules and part with Annie's address.

He could have killed her! Dennis may have fired the gun but he, Alex, had put her in danger—hadn't heeded the signs he'd known had been there and had stubbornly ploughed ahead in his own determined way, destroying all the safeguards she and her father had built up at such cost to their own lives.

He returned to Annie's room.

'It was my fault,' he said to Rod. 'My own stupid determination to find out more about her.'

He explained what he'd done, feeling more wretched every moment.

Rod said nothing for a while, then shook his head.

'Annie was worried she was putting *you* in danger,' he said. 'Thought she shouldn't go on seeing you because she was worried what would happen if Dennis ever found out.'

They sat in silence for a while, then Rod turned to Alex.

'Don't be so hard on yourself. Look at it this way. Annie's going to get better and we're finally rid of the black shadow Dennis cast over both our lives. Annie can still be Annie Talbot if she wants, but she can go visit her gran and get back with her family and never live in fear again. On top of that, you saved my life. He said he'd shoot me if I tried to warn Annie, and he meant it. If you hadn't come from nowhere and grabbed the chair, I'd be dead. We should be thanking you.'

'You can't possibly thank me for putting both of you in such danger,' Alex said hoarsely. 'And neither will she!'

He got up and left the room, wanting more than anything to be with Annie when she woke but feeling he'd forfeited the right. He went up to the unit and phoned the vet to learn that Henry was doing as well as could be expected, though it was still touch and go. Shock could do terrible things to a dog.

If Henry died…

No, Alex couldn't think about that. Surely he had enough guilt on his plate.

He wandered the corridors of the hospital for a while, unable to face the thought of going home, then eventually he made his way to the on-duty room where he'd spent so much time lately and lay down on the bed.

He had four days to get past this—to get his head together and be ready to face work again, face questions about what had happened to Annie. He'd have to talk to Rod again to work out how best to protect her. Probably have to talk to the police as well. He should do that now—see Rod first to discuss damage control. There was no way Annie would want details of her past plastered across the newspapers.

He got up off the bed and headed back to the second-floor room, where he and Rod made up a story they thought would be accepted.

'I've contacts in the police force over here,' Rod said. 'I'll make some phone calls, you stay here.'

'I can't stay here. She's never going to want to see me again when she learns what's happened.'

'She mightn't if you slink away like some lousy coward,' Rod said, 'but tell her face to face—that's different. And while I'm not a doctor, I don't think this is the time to say anything. Just let her get a bit better. Wait until she asks. You go blurting out a confession while she's still weak and confused, you'll make a hash of things for sure.'

He wheeled himself away and Alex was left standing sentinel beside the bed of the woman he loved.

'Sit down, you're in the way,' a nurse said minutes later, coming in to check on Annie's condition.

He sat, and when the nurse departed he took Annie's hand in his and started to tell her all the things he hadn't said about falling in love with her that night in Traders Rest and searching for her ever after, unable to believe his luck when he'd found her again.

He talked of love, and courage, and spread his dreams about the future out in front of her, knowing she couldn't hear him and that there might not be a future.

'And Henry's holding his own,' he said, when he'd unburdened all the secrets of his heart.

The fingers he held in his stirred, and a sleepy voice said, 'Henry?'

Alex could have cheered, but knew he'd wake the entire ward so contented himself with quiet reassurances.

'He's OK—he's at the vet's. I stayed for the operation and phoned just minutes ago. He's lost a lot of blood,' he added, because even a bullet-weakened Annie wasn't one to be taken in by false assurances. 'But the vet says he's holding his own.'

'And Dad?' Annie asked, her fingers turning to grip Alex's.

'He wasn't hurt. He's here at the hospital—he just left your side. Had to speak to some people.'

Annie opened her eyes and turned her head to look at Alex.

'Dad's unhurt because of you. I remember that part. You jumped the fence and pushed him away just before Dennis fired the gun. He'd have shot Dad—could have shot you.'

Tears welled in her eyes and she shook her head.

'I knew it couldn't be, Alex. Knew I was putting you in danger just by knowing you. I tried to tell you, but I loved you and couldn't push you away—not hard or far enough to keep you safe.'

The tears were spilling on the pillow and breaking Alex's heart.

'Annie, darling, it wasn't you who put me in danger, but me who did this to you. Please, don't blame yourself. Please, don't cry. I'm not worthy of your tears.'

She sniffed and brushed her free hand across her cheek.

'Not worthy—that's nonsense. If anyone's not worthy, it's me.'

Then her eyes widened and she looked apprehensively towards the door.

'Dennis?' she whispered, so hoarsely fearful Alex himself turned to make sure there wasn't a dead man standing in the doorway.

'He killed himself, Annie. He's dead.'

Alex watched the emotions chase each other across her face—disbelief, amazement, a little sadness and finally relief.

'I wouldn't have wished him dead,' she said quietly. 'But it's for the best.'

Then she closed her eyes and Alex let her rest, knowing she had many memories of the past to finally put to rest—knowing she had to become used to not living in fear.

CHAPTER THIRTEEN

ANNIE lay in the spa, looking out through the trees to the view of cliffs and gullies. The water bubbled around her, relaxing tired muscles and warming her body. It had been a long month, recuperating and getting Henry better. Then there'd been so much red tape to be sorted and often cut through. But they'd managed and yesterday Rowena Drake had married Alex Attwood, though it was Annie Talbot—no, Annie Attwood—who lay in the spa, waiting for her husband of a little over twenty-four hours to join her.

'OK?' he asked, as he dropped his robe and slid into the water, settling beside her and putting his arm around her shoulders.

'OK doesn't come near it, Alex,' she said, resting her head against his shoulder and nuzzling a kiss into his neck. 'OK isn't on the same continent as the way I'm feeling.'

'So tell me,' he suggested.

Annie shook her head, but because he'd come to know her so well he persisted.

'Come on—we're talkers, you and I. We tell each other things. That's the rule!'

'Your rule—and you just made it up.'

'I did,' Alex said smugly, 'but we're newly-weds, we can make up whatever rules we like for our marriage. I've thought of another one. Twenty kisses before breakfast—every day for the rest of our lives.'

Annie laughed.

'The way we kiss, it'd be dinnertime before we ate.'

She turned to kiss him to prove her point, and it was a long time before either of them spoke.

But one thing she'd learned about Alex was his persistence so, although his voice showed a fair degree of breathlessness from the kiss, he repeated his earlier demand.

'Tell me!'

Annie watched the tops of the trees that grew in the gully beneath the cabin sway in the breeze and saw the way the patterns of sky changed as the leaves moved.

'I feel new—reborn. I know that sounds silly, but I can't help feeling Annie Attwood is such a different person from the other people I've been.'

She turned and looked into the serious grey eyes of the man she loved.

'I have no fear, Alex. None at all. I was lying here in the spa, testing out all the bits of my body, and, no, there's no sign of it anywhere. And it's not just because Dennis is dead, but because of you. You've offered me a whole new life, and the thought of the two of us being together, of what we can do, the fun we can have, the joy we can share—it's blotted out the past completely.'

'No shadows?' Alex asked, tracing his thumb across her cheek, stroking the freckles he seemed so fascinated by.

'Not a one,' she assured him, and kissed him again to prove it.

Alex held her close. It had taken a while to get his Annie to the cabin in the mountains, but they'd finally made it. Made it in the most glorious way—in celebration of their marriage. And now Annie was truly his, in every way.

He drew her closer, feeling the softness of her body against his, feeling love in such overwhelming abundance he knew it would keep them both safe for ever.

'I love you, Annie Attwood,' he whispered, and kissed her once again, thinking how wide an arc they'd travelled since the first kiss they'd shared.

MEDICAL ROMANCE™

 *Large Print*

Titles for the next six months…

December

THE DOCTOR'S SPECIAL TOUCH   Marion Lennox
CRISIS AT KATOOMBA HOSPITAL   Lucy Clark
THEIR VERY SPECIAL MARRIAGE   Kate Hardy
THE HEART SURGEON'S PROPOSAL   Meredith Webber

January

THE CELEBRITY DOCTOR'S PROPOSAL Sarah Morgan
UNDERCOVER AT CITY HOSPITAL Carol Marinelli
A MOTHER FOR HIS FAMILY   Alison Roberts
A SPECIAL KIND OF CARING   Jennifer Taylor

February

HOLDING OUT FOR A HERO   Caroline Anderson
HIS UNEXPECTED CHILD   Josie Metcalfe
A FAMILY WORTH WAITING FOR   Margaret Barker
WHERE THE HEART IS   Kate Hardy

MILLS & BOON®

Live the emotion

1105 LP 2P P1 Medic

MEDICAL ROMANCE™

Large Print

March

THE ITALIAN SURGEON	Meredith Webber
A NURSE'S SEARCH AND RESCUE	Alison Roberts
THE DOCTOR'S SECRET SON	Laura MacDonald
THE FOREVER ASSIGNMENT	Jennifer Taylor

April

BRIDE BY ACCIDENT	Marion Lennox
COMING HOME TO KATOOMBA	Lucy Clark
THE CONSULTANT'S SPECIAL RESCUE	Joanna Neil
THE HEROIC SURGEON	Olivia Gates

May

THE NURSE'S CHRISTMAS WISH	Sarah Morgan
THE CONSULTANT'S CHRISTMAS PROPOSAL	
	Kate Hardy
NURSE IN A MILLION	Jennifer Taylor
A CHILD TO CALL HER OWN	Gill Sanderson

MILLS & BOON®

Live the emotion

1105 LP 2P P2 Medical